023
REKI KAWAHARA
abec
bee-pee
SWORD ART ONLINE
unital ring II

SAO
SWORD ART ONLINE

"Gwoeaaah!"

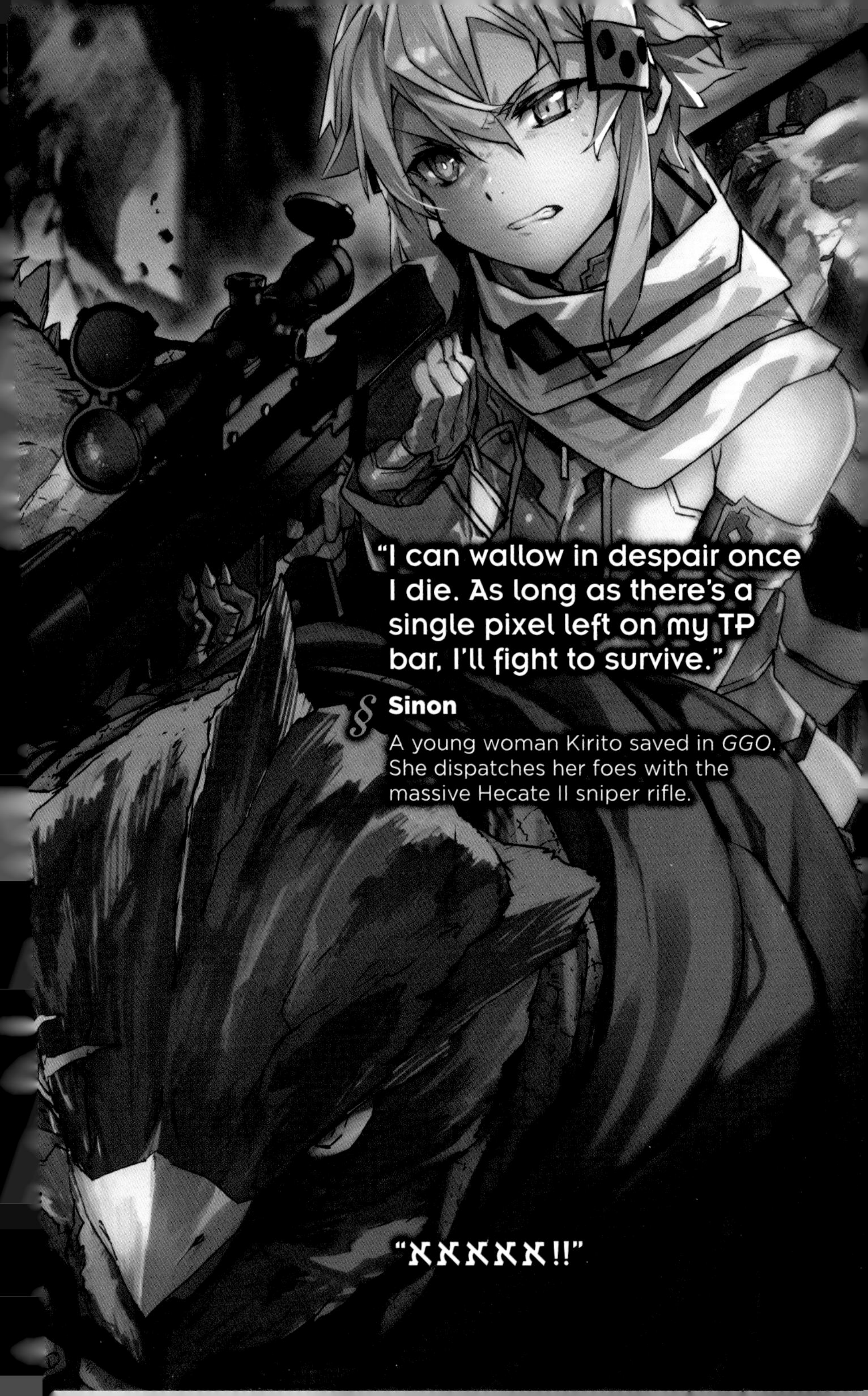
"I can wallow in despair once I die. As long as there's a single pixel left on my TP bar, I'll fight to survive."
§ Sinon
A young woman Kirito saved in GGO. She dispatches her foes with the massive Hecate II sniper rifle.
"אאאאא!!"

"...Sorry I haven't been in touch for a while, A-chan."
§ Argo
A talented info dealer and former beta tester of *SAO*, commonly known as Argo the Rat. Her whereabouts were unknown after the game ended, until...

"I knew...I *knew* I would see you again one day."
§ **Asuna Yuuki**
Kirito's girlfriend. She has been attending the same returnee school as him ever since *SAO* ended. Even in *Unital Ring*, she uses a rapier.

"Rgh...!"
§ Alice
An Integrity Knight of the Underworld and the world's first true bottom-up artificial intelligence. Her weapon in *Unital Ring* is a bastard sword.

§ Kirito
The boy who beat *SAO* and brought peace to the Underworld.
"Asuna...Silica...Alice!"
"We've got to protect our home!"

"The seeds bud, sprout stems and leaves, and join ends to form a circular gate.

Visitors to this land, drained of hope, preserve your solitary life.

Withstand myriad trials, survive untold dangers,

and to the first to reach the land revealed by the heavenly light, all shall be given."

Unital Ring is an open-world survival game made by the fusion of all the VRMMOs built with the Seed program, including *ALO* and *GGO*.

Its full scope is still shrouded in mystery, but the message from the disembodied voice says that the point of the game is to be the first player to reach "the land revealed by the heavenly light."

All you can bring from your pre-fusion game are your two weapons with the longest usage times, one skill with the highest proficiency level, and your currently equipped armor. Everything else, including player stats and items, is completely reset.

In terms of gameplay, it adds a player-level system that did not exist in *ALO* and the parameters of TP (thirst points) and SP (stamina points). If TP or SP gets to zero, HP will begin to decrease, and if they all reach zero, the player is dead. If you die, you can never log in to *Unital Ring* again.

Illustration: Reki Kawahara

VOLUME 23

Reki Kawahara

abec

bee-pee

New York

SWORD ART ONLINE, Volume 23: UNITAL RING II
REKI KAWAHARA

Translation by Stephen Paul
Cover art by abec

SWORD ART ONLINE Vol.23

Edited by Dengeki Bunko
First published in Japan in 2019 by KADOKAWA CORPORATION, Tokyo.
English translation rights arranged with KADOKAWA CORPORATION, Tokyo, through Tuttle-Mori Agency, Inc., Tokyo.

Yen On
150 30th Street, 19th Floor
New York, NY 10001

Visit us at yenpress.com
facebook.com/yenpress
twitter.com/yenpress
yenpress.tumblr.com
instagram.com/yenpress

First Yen On Edition: October 2021

Yen On is an imprint of Yen Press, LLC.
The Yen On name and logo are trademarks of Yen Press, LLC.

Library of Congress Cataloging-in-Publication Data
Names: Kawahara, Reki, author. | Abec, 1985– illustrator. | Paul, Stephen, translator.
Title: Sword art online / Reki Kawahara, abec ; translation, Stephen Paul.
Description: First Yen On edition. | New York, NY : Yen On, 2014–
Identifiers: LCCN 2014001175 | ISBN 9780316371247 (v. 1 : pbk.) |
ISBN 9780316376815 (v. 2 : pbk.) | ISBN 9780316296427 (v. 3 : pbk.) |
ISBN 9780316296434 (v. 4 : pbk.) | ISBN 9780316296441 (v. 5 : pbk.) |
ISBN 9780316296458 (v. 6 : pbk.) | ISBN 9780316390408 (v. 7 : pbk.) |
ISBN 9780316390415 (v. 8 : pbk.) | ISBN 9780316390422 (v. 9 : pbk.) |
ISBN 9780316390439 (v. 10 : pbk.) | ISBN 9780316390446 (v. 11 : pbk.) |
ISBN 9780316390453 (v. 12 : pbk.) | ISBN 9780316390460 (v. 13 : pbk.) |
ISBN 9780316390484 (v. 14 : pbk.) | ISBN 9780316390491 (v. 15 : pbk.) |
ISBN 9781975304188 (v. 16 : pbk.) | ISBN 9781975356972 (v. 17 : pbk.) |
ISBN 9781975356996 (v. 18 : pbk.) | ISBN 9781975357016 (v. 19 : pbk.) |
ISBN 9781975357030 (v. 20 : pbk.) | ISBN 9781975315955 (v. 21 : pbk.) |
ISBN 9781975321741 (v. 22 : pbk.) | ISBN 9781975321765 (v. 23 : pbk.)
Subjects: CYAC: Science fiction. | BISAC: FICTION / Science Fiction / Adventure.
Classification: pz7.K1755Ain 2014 | DDC [Fic]—dc23
LC record available at https://lccn.loc.gov/2014001175

ISBNs: 978-1-9753-2176-5 (paperback)
978-1-9753-2177-2 (ebook)

10 9 8 7 6 5 4 3 2 1

LSC-C

Printed in the United States of America

"THIS MIGHT BE A GAME, BUT IT'S NOT SOMETHING YOU PLAY."

—Akihiko Kayaba, *Sword Art Online* programmer

SWORD ART ONLINE
unital ring II

Reki Kawahara

abec

bee-pee

1

Thirst.

The sensation of thirst was so realistic, it was hard to believe it was just a simulation created by the AmuSphere. The tongue lost moisture, and the throat hurt with each breath. It made her wonder if her biological body, resting on her bed in the real world, was suffering from dehydration.

I wish I could log out and chug an entire glass of ice-cold water, she thought. But in this mysterious world, *Unital Ring*, her avatar would not vanish while she was away. Her thirst meter would stop, but if she logged off, drank water, and logged back in, the meter would still be depleted. And now that the grace period had ended, if she died once in *UR*, she could never log back in again. Potentially, she could lose her character and all of her items. That was the one thing she had to avoid.

And that was why Shino Asada, aka Sinon, was rushing desperately across the barren wasteland in search of water to quench her virtual thirst.

Running made the thirst meter deplete more quickly, but walking wouldn't get her there any faster, either. She just had to trust that if she ran far enough, she'd find a source of water before her TP hit zero. The desert was very flat overall, but about half a mile ahead, there was a small boulder with what looked like plants growing along its silhouette. If there wasn't water around there, she was out of ideas.

"Seriously...How could I let myself get stuck in this situation...?"

Her voice was hoarse in her parched throat. Sinon clicked her tongue, thinking about the mistakes in judgment that had led her here.

Six hours earlier, at 4:50 PM on Sunday, September 27th, 2026.

Sinon was logged in to the VRMMORPG *Gun Gale Online* (*GGO*), delving in a high-level dungeon and farming mechanical enemies for rare metal drops.

Since making an account for *ALfheim Online* (*ALO*), the home territory of her friends, she'd spent more time playing over there, but Sinon had no intention whatsoever of quitting *GGO*. The only weapon she'd ever used that was truly a part of her was the Hecate II, and she intended to win the next Bullet of Bullets tournament entirely on her own. Her solo metal farming was so that she could customize the Hecate and avoid the attention of her rivals in doing so.

The metal had only a 3 percent drop rate, and she was down to just one more to go when it happened:

The ground of the dungeon had rumbled beneath her feet, rainbow colors had filled her vision, and then she was teleported back to the surface.

She found herself in a town she'd never seen before. Weak sunlight coming through a thin cloud layer quietly illuminated a gray city. The road stretched in both directions without a soul in sight.

Sinon had traveled the world map of *GGO* from end to end, but she didn't recognize this place. The buildings were constructed not of concrete but of old-fashioned stone, and the road was paved with cracked bricks rather than asphalt. More and more *GGO* players teleported in around her, all of whom looked around in bewilderment. She didn't recognize a single one.

The situation was baffling, but Sinon did not appreciate being surrounded by unfamiliar men, so she stole away into a nearby building. Checking to make sure there were no residents inside, she hid in an upstairs room, clutching the Hecate to her chest as she listened to the voices outside.

About ten players gathered together and began to discuss what was happening in the hopes of finding an answer. Someone eventually noticed a fundamental change to the UI of the system menu, so they attempted to contact the development team but got no response.

That left logging out as the only option to collect more information. By now, there would be plenty of posts about this anomaly on *GGO* community sites and social media. Sinon really wanted to log out to learn more, but an ominous feeling kept her online.

Outside the building, the ten players were using their strange new menus to return to the real world. Once the outside area was silent again, Sinon leaned out the empty window to look at the road below, and gasped.

The ten avatars were still there, resting in the middle of the road on one knee. That was the standby pose, a familiar sight from *GGO* and *ALO*. In most VRMMOs, it was common practice to keep player avatars present in the world for several minutes after they logged off while outdoors to prevent them from being able to escape from monsters or other players by just turning off the game. If that rule still held true, it meant this city was considered "wilderness" rather than an actual city and offered no automatic protection. Then again, there were absolutely no civilians around, so you couldn't even call it a city—more of a ruin, really.

And that meant…

Sinon was watching the scene with her breath trapped in her lungs when she heard a kind of skittering, scraping sound. She looked to the right and saw a number of long, thin shadows emerging into the waning sunlight from a side path. They were insectoid monsters, like a cross between a centipede and an earwig, except they were about two and a half feet long.

Based on the size, they didn't seem to be that dangerous. But all the *GGO* players within their attention were offline at the moment. The gleaming assault rifles and laser guns on the players' backs were impressive, but they were useless without an active finger to pull the trigger.

"Come on—log back in!" she hissed, gripping the windowsill, but the ten of them just knelt there, perfectly still. The centipedes were rapidly approaching, their many legs skittering across the paving stones. Sinon reached behind her on pure instinct, grasping for the backup MP7 she kept in a holster.

But she stopped short. The five centipedes visible weren't necessarily the only ones nearby. Gunshots could potentially attract an entire swarm of them. She had a silencer on the MP7 for this very purpose, but she'd left it in item storage while she was farming for materials to maximize her carrying space. There was no time to dig through her menu so she could pull it out and snap it onto the muzzle.

While she sat there, paralyzed with indecision, the lead centipede crawled onto the back of one of the players and dug its huge jaws into his unprotected neck. Crimson damage effects spilled from the spot like spurting blood. The other centipedes quickly set upon the rest of the players.

Sinon assumed that, even as helpless as they were, the players could survive a few minutes of biting. The centipedes were obviously low-level monsters, and the men were outfitted with pretty fancy armor.

But just a matter of seconds later, the player who had been bitten first simply emitted blue particles and vanished. The other players died shortly after him. It happened all too quickly. Either the centipedes were much tougher than Sinon thought or…

Sinon opened the strange ring menu. Out of the eight icons there, she touched the human-shaped one, which she guessed was her status window. When she saw the values that appeared, she gasped.

Level-1. Maximum HP, just 200. Her stats had been reinitialized.

That wasn't all. Below her white HP bar was a green MP bar,

then a blue bar marked TP, and a yellow bar marked SP. MP was easy enough, but she had no idea what SP and TP were supposed to represent.

There was no point trying to figure that out now, though. She glanced out the window again—five players were gone. The other five still living were now in the centipedes' sights. They were going to be wiped out before any of them returned.

"Ugh...!"

Sinon drew her MP7. She unfolded the foregrip, extended the stock, and switched the selector from safety to semi-auto. Pulling the cocking lever loaded the first bullet into the chamber, and she took aim at the lead centipede, resting her body against the windowsill. Her finger slid against the trigger and tensed just a little.

"Huh...?"

She was aghast. One of the two major systems that made *GGO*, well, *GGO* was nowhere to be seen: the bullet circle.

A bug? A system error? Or...? There was no time to wonder. Some monsters had the ability to nullify the bullet circle, forcing you to use your sights and aim the traditional way. She was shooting down from the second floor, but at this distance, there was no real concern about the trajectory being off.

Sinon aimed at the head of the centipede as it prepared to bite its new target, then double-tapped. Its reddish-black shell burst, shooting sticky green fluid outward. The second shot missed by a bit, but an HP bar with an unfamiliar shape over the centipede's head rapidly dwindled to zero. The centipede screeched with its final breath, curled backward, and fell to the street, then...did *not* burst into blue shards and disappear. It was still there, but it was definitely dead.

She tried to aim for the next centipede and clicked her tongue. There were red cursors over the heads of the other four creatures. Her instincts told her they were focused on her now, and that was correct. They changed direction to approach her building. She told herself not to panic and took out a second centipede with another double-tap.

The remaining three immediately scurried straight up the stone wall. She switched the selector to full auto and leaned out the window to aim downward. The rhythm of the gunfire was pleasing, and a third centipede fell to the ground, ooze pouring from its carapace where the 4.6 mm bullets struck it.

The fourth met the same fate as the others, but the fifth reached the window. Sharp mandibles extended from its mouth toward her, and it swung its pincer bottom to point at her, too.

Sinon didn't force her shot, kicking off the sill instead. She did a backflip as she flew and opened fire with the MP7 when she landed. It cracked the fifth centipede's head as the insect tried to get inside the building. Its long, thin torso hung over the sill.

"Whew," she exhaled, checking the remaining ammo in her magazine out of sheer habit.

A sudden, unfamiliar musical fanfare blared in her ears, and a blue ring rose from her feet up over her head. A window popped up in front of her.

Sinon's level has risen to 2.

"Level-2..."

She couldn't help but repeat it like a lament. In *GGO* three days ago, Sinon had just reached level-107. Once Zaskar, the dev team for *GGO*, realized the error, they would probably do a server rollback for everyone, but the game map and monsters were too polished for this to be some kind of glitch. It was like she'd been tossed out of *GGO* and pulled into a completely different game...

With her MP7 still at the ready, Sinon carefully walked toward the centipede's body. She poked it with the muzzle a few times, but it did not move. After that, she took her hand off the foregrip and tapped the creature with a finger.

A properties window appeared with a *shwam* sound. It said: *Red-bellied Centiwig Corpse, Material, Weight: 5.82.*

The *red-bellied* part of the name made sense. The red coloring on its underside was brighter than on its back. And if it was classified as a material, that suggested something.

Sinon put the MP7 back in its holster and reached for the knife on her belt. But she touched nothing. She looked down at her right side and saw that the space where she kept her favorite survival knife was empty.

"..."

She glanced in confusion at the Hecate II resting against the wall. She had her main weapon and her side weapon, plus all her armor, so why would her knife be the one thing missing? Maybe it fell out when she did the backflip—not that such a thing should ever happen—but there was no sign of it around the room. She did, however, notice a cabinet against the wall.

On closer examination, the cabinet was unlike the metal cabinet style of the world of *GGO*. It was an old-fashioned wooden cabinet, more suited to the world of Alfheim, if anything. She opened the grimy old doors and found almost nothing inside except for some broken dishes, a bottle filled with an unidentifiable substance, and one small knife.

She picked up the knife. It was not meant for combat; at best, it was suited for peeling fruit, but the blade still had a little bit of an edge, at least. With the rusty knife in her hand, she went back to the centipede. After much hesitation, she jammed the knife into the gap between its segments.

There was a skin-crawling *chugk* sound and a vibration in her hand that made her want to hurl the knife away—but fortunately, one action was all it took for the centipede's body to flash blue and vanish. A number of items fell on the spot it had occupied.

A message appeared reading *Dismantling skill gained. Proficiency has risen to 1.*

She shrugged and minimized it. On the ground were a couple of reddish-black plates and what looked like two curved thorns. She scooped them up and tapped them, turning them into *Inferior Centipede Carapace* and *Inferior Centipede Pincers*. She didn't know what they were for, but it couldn't hurt to have them. Sinon opened her menu and tossed the carapace and pincers into her inventory. Then she stuck the knife into her belt, picked up the Hecate II, and left the room to head back down.

From the entrance of the building, she peered outside. She'd blasted the gun at full auto, but no new centipedes or other monsters seemed to be emerging.

The five players she'd saved were still in their standby poses. She used her knife to dismantle the four other centipede bodies and claim their materials.

"Can't upgrade the Hecate with centipede shells, I assume," Sinon muttered, sighing once again. However, she soon noticed that there were five dark bags resting on the ground where the player avatars had died earlier.

"..."

Feeling hesitant, she approached, sticking the knife back into her belt and touching one of the bags. It turned into a ring of light and disappeared. There was a new message for her now:

AK-47M acquired. Tactical Vest acquired.

"..."

Both were standard equipment in *GGO*. As she expected, the contents of the black bags belonged to the dead players. Of course, it was the centipedes that had killed the players, not Sinon, but looting a dead player wasn't her style. She was opening her inventory to put the items back when she noticed something.

In basically every VRMMO, items left behind in the world would vanish after a certain amount of time. She wasn't sure where the respawn point would be for those players, but once they realized their weapons had dropped, they'd be rushing back to reclaim them. If she wanted to be considerate, she should hold on to them until the players returned.

So she decided not to materialize the first items she'd looted, and she picked up the other four bags. She was worried about storage space, so she checked her window again, but her carrying capacity wasn't even at 20 percent.

Struck with foreboding, she checked the contents and saw that all she was carrying were ten retrieved items and the materials from the centipedes. All of the items she had earned in *GGO* were gone.

"Unbelievable..."

She closed the window.

Her items would probably come back once the situation was resolved, but it was worrying that there was still no announcement from the dev team. She wanted to avoid losing her Hecate and MP7 if she died, so it seemed like she'd have to make her precious guns last until the rollback could begin—and then another thought made her suck in a breath through her teeth.

If everything in her inventory was gone, that meant her healthy stock of 12.7 mm ammo for the Hecate and 4.6 mm ammo for the MP7 was gone, too. The only things left were the seven shots in the Hecate's magazine and the forty or so bullets between the MP7 and its magazine on her belt. Once she'd fired them all, the only weapon Sinon would have left would be the rusty kitchen knife she'd found in the cabinet of the abandoned home.

Strictly speaking, she also had the weapons and ammo dropped by the five dead players. But if she made off with them, she was nothing but a looter in name and fact.

Belatedly, she regretted using her guns on the centipedes at the full auto setting. Still, Sinon waited for the other five to log in again. The centipedes would be back eventually, so the six of them had to work together to survive. She pulled the MP7 from her holster again, then backed against the wall of the building and waited for three minutes.

At last, one of the players twitched, then bolted to his feet.

"Hey, everybody, let's move! In the middle of the ruins is...," he shouted but stopped when he noticed that only Sinon was present and listening. He looked around, then lowered his voice and said, "Hey, you, there were about five more people here before, right? You know where they went?"

"They died, unfortunately," she said, shrugging.

Sinon was about to explain about the centipede attack when the player—who was dressed in gray digital camo and used an optical gun—took aim at her with the assault rifle on his shoulder.

"So you're a PKer, huh?!"

"What?!" she shouted, a mixture of surprise and outrage. Then she realized that what she said could be interpreted as a bit of creative assassin role-playing. Plus, she had the MP7 in her hand, so she quickly lowered it and protested, "No, it wasn't me—it was giant centipedes!"

"Oh yeah? And where are they?!"

"I took them out! I saved your lives!" Sinon objected. She wanted to open her window so she could take out the carapaces to prove it to him, but the man immediately pulled the trigger and left a burn mark on the wall just to the right of Sinon with a yellowish-green laser.

"Hey!!"

"Don't move! Only the lowest of the low would prey on people while they're logged out!"

"I'm not preying on anyone!" she hissed, trying to suppress her anger. But the man was in a rage and wouldn't take his finger off the trigger. If she tried to move again, he would hit her for certain. Sinon was only level-1—well, level-2—so even a low-powered optical rifle could kill her instantly. If she died and dropped the Hecate, the man would assume it was rightfully his, won in battle.

Should she take the initiative and kill him first to protect her partner? But how?

A new voice broke the silent tension.

"Damn, this is crazy! It's not just *GGO*," shouted one of the other players as he got to his feet. When he noticed the man with the gun and Sinon, he exaggeratedly leaned backward in shock. "Wh-whoa, what are you doing, man?"

"Use your brain! This chick killed five of us while we were offline!"

"Yikes!"

The second man pulled a large-caliber revolver—probably a Ruger Blackhawk—from his holster. Sinon's back was literally against the wall, and while she was searching for a way out, the other three awakened in quick order.

She'd completely lost the chance for initiative. It seemed the only thing she could do now was pray that one of these people would be calm and hear her out.

Then a familiar dry skittering hit her ears. She looked around briefly and saw two long antennae extending from a split off the road, to the left behind the men. The antennae just wavered there for a moment, then emerged farther, attached to a head with huge mandibles and a long body. The red-bellied centiwigs had respawned.

Because the guy with the optical gun was screaming his head off, the others didn't realize the danger. She rolled her eyes yet again and muttered quietly, "Behind you."

"What?! Did you say something?!" her assailant growled.

Again, she warned, "Behind you!"

"What, you think I'm gonna fall for the oldest trick in the book? Hurry up and drop your loot before I shoot—"

But a shriek—"Aaaiiieee!"—interrupted him.

"What the hell was that for? Would you shut up…?" the rifleman snapped, glancing over his shoulder, only to let out a yelp. "Gwah?!"

At last, he'd noticed the centipedes emerging onto the road. There were at least ten of them.

The five brigands backed away, guns aimed.

This is it…I have to escape now. The red-bellied centiwigs looked frightening, but two or three 4.6 mm bullets from the MP7 were all it took to kill them. The players' gear was at least mid-rank, so if they shot like hell, it would take less than a minute for them to kill the bugs.

The instant she heard the first shot, Sinon bolted. She put the MP7 back into its holster and sprinted in the opposite direction of the gunfire. It was strange that she could run perfectly fine with the ultraheavy Hecate II on her back, despite being only level-2, but she wouldn't know why unless she survived this situation.

In less than five seconds, she heard an angry shout among the gunfire.

"Ah! Hey, the chick ran away!"

"Dammit! Let's finish them off and go after her!"

At that point, she was rooting for the centipedes to put up a better fight. This left her with maybe ten seconds to get away from the wide-open main street.

Right after he'd logged back in, the optical rifleman had said, *Hey, everybody, let's move! In the middle of the ruins is...* The most straightforward interpretation of that statement would be *In the middle of the ruins is a safe space.* So she wanted to head that way, but it was difficult to go to a place with lots of players around if some of them assumed she was a PKer. So she should head for somewhere *outside* the ruined town.

Sinon recalled what she'd seen looking out the upstairs window. In her memory, the direction across from the window—meaning the left side of where she was running—featured a group of larger buildings. If that was the center of town, then the right-hand side was the way to leave.

The gunshots were wrapping up in the background. She had to get away from the main road before the men spotted her. Side street, side street...There. Five yards ahead.

Sinon tilted herself as far as she could go and made a ninety-degree turn down the side path as close as possible without slipping and tumbling. There was a narrow alley barely four feet wide between the buildings. If it was a dead end, she was screwed; she just had to have faith for now.

As she ran, stepping as lightly as possible, she saw three half-broken wooden boxes up ahead. She jumped behind them and crouched. In less than ten seconds, she could hear the stomping of heavy combat boots as well as irritated exclamations.

"Damn! Where'd that girl go?!"

"Maybe she snuck into one of the houses or down a side alley?"

"So we have to go searching them one by one? Man..."

"Don't complain! She killed five of us!"

"Plus, that chick's sni-ri was superrare. If it doesn't get rolled back, we could sell it and split the winnings and *still* all come out superrich."

...*What the hell is a sni-ri?* she wondered, then realized it was supposed to be an abbreviation of *sniper rifle*. They were right that the Hecate II was one of the rarest weapons in *GGO*, but if she lost it to scrubs who would call it something as stupid as a sni-ri and then sell it for cash, she'd never live that down.

If the men came down the alley in a line, she'd just have to shoot through all five of them with one of the Hecate's 12.7 mm bullets. But doing that, even in self-defense, made her a true PKer. Plus, she had only seven bullets left, and she didn't want to have to use them on this.

Don't come down here! she begged.

It was as though they could hear her mind. The footsteps slowed at the entrance to the alley. She couldn't see them, but she could sense their attention on the spot where she was hiding.

Sinon silently slipped the Hecate off her back and held it in both hands. Now she wished she'd left one more bullet in the chamber for good measure. She placed her right hand on the bolt handle. She'd wait for them to come down the alley as close as possible before loading the bullet, and then she had to shoot before they reacted to the sound.

One, two...three seconds later.

"Hey, someone check those busted crates..."

But she didn't hear the rest because it was drowned out by the burst of a submachine gun. Live bullets burst through the wooden boxes, grazing Sinon's hair and combat boots. Her instincts screamed at her to bolt from the hiding spot, but through sheer willpower, she kept her avatar still.

"Nothing there."

"Don't just start shooting like that, man!"

The first voice merely laughed. Five sets of footsteps moved away, but Sinon stayed in place for another thirty seconds before carefully rising. The wooden boxes were torn up after getting shot, and one more impact would have crumbled them to splinters.

You're going to regret wasting those bullets, she warned them silently, then rushed down the other end of the alley.

* * *

Fortunately, the narrow path wasn't a dead end, and it took her to another, larger street. Once upon a time, many people must have walked the stone-paved road that now hosted little more than wind and dust. What had turned this town into an empty ruin? The answer might lie in the center, but she wasn't going there anytime soon.

Sinon headed for the outward edge of the town, realizing that at some point, she had stopped thinking of this place as a glitch or an unintended case of human error but as a proper VRMMO world with its own internal logic. She encountered the occasional centipede, spider, and scorpion-type monster, but she chose to conserve her limited ammo and ran away from them. At this point, she wished she could have switched her side weapon from the MP7 to a photon sword...but hindsight was twenty-twenty.

She was on the move for over twenty minutes, avoiding battle, when a tall stone wall came into view. It looked very much like a castle wall surrounding a city, but it was stacked with seamless blocks, with no way of climbing up them.

Sinon grabbed a pebble and flicked it upward with her thumb. When it landed on the ground, it bounced to the right, so she followed the wall in that direction.

In less than a minute, she arrived at a large gate. Praying that it wasn't locked, she approached carefully, but she soon saw that her worries were unfounded. The heavy wooden double gate was standing on one side, but the other side had come out of the frame and fallen to the ground.

She stopped, wondering if leaving the town was really better than staying. But there was no way to know the right answer; the only thing she knew for sure was that she couldn't approach the other *GGO* players who had been teleported here until she cleared up their misconception that she was a PKer.

What she needed now was a safe place where she could log out. If there were centipedes and scorpions and such all over town, the only possible shelter she'd find was outside.

With her mind made up for now, Sinon walked up to the gate, stepped through the empty frame, and made her way outside the city.

"......Whoa..."

Instantly, she found herself gasping at the view spread out before her.

The scale of the world map was, simply put, *vast.*

GGO's familiar world was anything but cramped. On foot, walking across the wasteland surrounding the capital of SBC Glocken took over five hours. But this mysterious world wasn't just vast—it was incredibly detailed. Every VR world naturally faded out as you gazed into the far distance, but the dried earth here just continued on and on toward the horizon until it met ranges of distant mountains that were still crystal clear to the eye. She hadn't felt this much of a sense of scale since her dive into that *true* alternate reality, the Underworld.

Unconsciously, Sinon raised her hand and touched the side of her head. It wasn't here now, but back in the real world, where she was lying on her bed, she was wearing the AmuSphere she'd been using for close to a year and a half. It wasn't the latest and greatest piece of gear anymore. How was it creating such a vivid experience?

She needed to log out soon and find out what was happening. Sinon blinked, switching gears in her mind, and stared at the wilderness under the afternoon sun with renewed attention.

The terrain was about 70 percent dry, sandy ground and 30 percent faded plants, with the occasional cactus rising above it all. It reminded her of the Sonoran Desert in Mexico, not that she'd ever been there, though.

There were monsters, too. Just from here, she could make out two giant scorpions and one giant lizard. It wasn't going to be easy to look for safety while avoiding the predators' reaction range. But then she finally remembered something. The Hecate's precious bullets needed to be conserved, but there was more her gun could do than just shoot holes in things.

Sinon assumed a standing firing position with the Hecate and looked through its scope, turning the dial until its magnification was at 5×, the lowest it offered. Then she moved the gun slowly from left to right, searching for safe ground.

It seemed like being close to the ground wouldn't help. She needed to find a high space where the scorpions and lizards couldn't reach her, with cover she could hide behind.

But it was unlikely she'd find such a convenient spot here, so she'd settle for a raised area with a flat top…

"……Ah," she grunted.

Sinon pulled away from the scope, then looked through it again, raising the magnification to 10×. She'd found a tall gray rocky pillar jutting from the desert floor. It was pointed on the top, but there was something like a cave near the base. If she could climb her way up there, it would be the perfect shelter. And the distance was reasonable, no more than half a mile at the most.

She lowered her gun, steeled herself for action, and stepped down off the fallen door. The soles of her boots hit dry dirt, slightly scraping the ground with every step. She wouldn't be returning to this city for a while. She had to survive on her own until this strange situation sorted itself out.

At about thirty feet, she broke into a measured run. When she saw monsters ahead of her, she went well out of her way and kept an eye on the distant rocky point beyond the brush.

Thankfully, she didn't have to contend with any scorpions or lizards up close before she reached her destination. Seen from the base, the rocky pillar was about fifty feet tall. The sides were nearly vertical. It seemed like only the centipedes from the town would be able to climb something like that—until she noticed the cracks and handholds on the rock surface. Sinon flexed her hands for a bit as she charted out a path up to the cave entrance. Once she had one, she grabbed the first handhold, jammed the toe of her boot into a crack, and pulled herself up.

In *GGO*—and probably in real life—a sniper's success was

largely defined by how much elevation they could gain, so free-climbing was a regular part of her work. The trick to rock climbing in a VRMMO was to do it fast, before the fatigue variable kicked in. She quickly got about fifteen feet up the surface.

Climbing skill gained. Proficiency has risen to 1.

The sudden message, right in front of her eyes, caused her to miss the next hold she was aiming for. Her weight slid, but her left hand caught a small gap at the last moment, preventing her from falling. She clicked her tongue with annoyance and closed the window, then resumed climbing.

Thankfully, that single point of proficiency in the Climbing skill helped, because she was able to reach the cave entrance without further trouble. It was a dark hole about two feet around, and she had to be careful to slip inside without catching the Hecate on the sides. In the real world, a hole like this might end up too shallow to be of use, but in a game, the devs never put things like this in unless it was worth the trouble.

As she expected, the cave widened as it got deeper. That increased the chances it was a monster's lair, so she slipped the MP7 out of its holster and turned on the small flashlight she had attached to a mount on her right side. Its white light cut through the darkness.

The cave was shaped like a cocoon, about four and a half feet tall and ten feet deep. There were no monsters here, nor any nest materials around her feet. Instead, there was a single wooden box with a reinforced metal frame along the back wall.

"……A treasure chest?" Sinon murmured, approaching in a crouch. She tapped the lid with the gun's muzzle, and it made a hard, heavy sound. The chest didn't look weathered or aged at all, in the sense of being left behind for years and years, so in her mind, that made it more likely that it was a treasure chest. She *had* to open it. As Sinon reached out with her left hand, she noticed a keyhole in the metal facing on the front.

She tried to lift the lid anyway, but it might as well have been glued in place. She exhaled and peered through the keyhole.

GGO's treasure chests—or treasure boxes, as players called them in-game—were usually locked. There were electronic locks and physical locks, and sometimes the boxes could have both, meaning you needed both the Lock-Picking and Hacking skills. If it was just a physical lock, she could attempt shooting it with her gun, but the chances of success were low when you did that. More often than not, you just permanently broke the latch or destroyed the contents of the box.

Sinon looked back and forth from the MP7 to the keyhole but successfully resisted the allure of the gamble. If she wasted a valuable bullet and destroyed the chest, too, she'd feel like a total failure. She would have tried picking the lock, but all of her lock-picking tools were gone, along with the rest of her stuff. All she had were the belongings of the unfortunate men, a rusty knife, and some centipede mats.

"..."

However, a curious idea came to her. Sinon opened the ring menu and hesitantly found her way to the EQUIPMENT icon. From her very inadequate list, she selected *Inferior Centipede Pincers* and materialized one.

A reddish-black pincer six inches long appeared. The two sharp, curved spikes were connected at the base. If she held them in both hands, she could work them back and forth, but she couldn't begin to guess what the pincers were meant to be crafted into. The only thing that mattered now, however, was that they were sharp.

Sinon stuck the pointed end of one of the spikes into the keyhole, then moved it around gently until there was a feeling of catching on something. It wasn't as effective as a proper lockpick, but she supposed that if the chest was ranked low enough, this was a worthwhile substitute.

She dug the spike around, trying to move whatever it was caught on, and a new message appeared.

Lock-Picking skill gained. Proficiency has risen to 1.

So it seemed there were a ton of various skills in this world.

There was no way this situation could just be a system error at this point, but she had to focus on the lock and ignore the bigger questions.

"Grrr...stupid...thing...," she hissed under her breath, tweaking the lock for a good three minutes. But when another message finally appeared telling her the Lock-Picking skill's proficiency had risen to 2, there was a pleasant clicking sound. That was also the moment the durability of the centipede's pincer ran out, and it crumbled in her hand.

Holding her breath, Sinon lifted the lid of the chest. It creaked ever so slightly and revealed a handful of coins, an aged leather bag, and one greenish rusted key.

She picked up a coin, the only silver of the bunch, and examined it closely. It was a circle about three-quarters of an inch across, and it was neither the credits of *GGO* nor the yrd of *ALO*. On one side was the number *100*, and on the back was an image of two trees. She tapped it to bring up a properties window that said *100-el Silver Coin, Currency, Weight: 0.1.*

"El...?"

She'd never heard of that currency. She shrugged and deposited the silver coin and the other copper coins into her inventory. Next, she took out the rusted key. There was an ornate openwork flower pattern on the handle, but she had no idea where this fancy key was supposed to go. She gave it a tap, too. *Bronze Key, Tool, Weight: 0.72.* No information of use.

Sinon tossed the key into her inventory next and saved the leather bag for last. It was tantalizingly heavy. Maybe it was full of gold coins, unlike the inside of the chest itself. Or perhaps there was a magical item inside. She widened the mouth of the bag and stuck her hand inside. Her fingers brushed against a couple of round items, so she pulled one out.

"...What is this?"

Resting in her palm was something like a metal ball bearing, small and shining. Its dark surface felt like iron or lead. It didn't look valuable. She peered into the bag and saw that all the items were the same. Sinon was disappointed, but she tapped the metal ball anyway to see its properties.

Crude Musket Ball, Weapon/Bullet, Attack Power: 28.42 puncturing, Weight: 3.67.

"They're just bullets..."

So the treasure chests that popped up in the middle of the wilderness could only be so good. Disappointed, she nearly tossed the iron ball aside before she stopped herself.

"...Musket ball?"

Was there a category for that kind of ammo in *GGO*?

From what Sinon knew, muskets were extremely primitive flintlock guns that were muzzle-loaded. They were long guns, but they weren't rifles, because their barrels did not have rifling lines cut into the inside. They were only one step forward from matchlocks.

The setting of *GGO* was a once-advanced world that had fallen into ruin after a civilization-ending war, with all of the sophisticated metalworking knowledge lost. Humanity could just barely manufacture optical guns, which were mostly made of plastic, and live-ammo guns, which required metal stamping and machining, were completely beyond even the most capable NPC. The live-ammo guns could be salvaged only from the prewar ruins. Sinon's Hecate II and MP7 were both items she'd looted from the dungeon beneath the capital city.

But the guns excavated from the ruins were from the early twentieth century at the oldest. She'd never heard of anyone pulling a seventeenth-century musket out of a dungeon. You'd have to pack in a new bullet and gunpowder after every shot, so even shooting at the weakest monster would be a big pain in the ass.

Meaning...

"There are muskets in this world...?" Sinon muttered, examining the iron ball again. Seconds later, she put it back into the bag, closed the bag tight, and put it into her inventory.

So I didn't find any proper treasure, but at least I managed to open the chest itself, she told herself, leaning against a gently curved wall. It was six PM. There weren't going to be any monsters here, she decided. Time to log out and figure out what was going on.

But before that, a break. She'd wait around for five minutes, or maybe just three, and be certain she was safe first. Once offline, she could replenish her fluids and eat something small...*What do I have in the refrigerator, again?* She still had some pork miso soup from last night. She could reheat that, then cook one of the millet dumplings her grandmother sent...

Sinon didn't even realize her eyes were closed until she sank to the bottom of warm darkness.

She thought she heard an odd noise.

It was like the ringing of countless bells in the far distance, or of shards of glass gently falling and piling up. Something delicate and beautiful.

Her eyebrows worked themselves several times before her eyes finally opened. She was looking not at the white wallpaper of her room but at a rough stone surface. For an instant, she didn't recognize where she was, until she realized she had fallen asleep in the virtual cave without logging off.

The time readout said it was 9:05 PM. She'd been asleep for three hours. That meant there was no automatic deconnecting system here that would log out players detected to have fallen asleep. Then again, maybe she was lucky; if the game had cut her off, she might have been comfortable enough in her real body in bed that she'd have slept eight hours instead.

In any case, the strange, continuous sound was drawing her attention toward the mouth of the little cave.

Her sleepiness dissipated in an instant.

There was a brilliant purple light shining into the cave from the outside, which should have been well past nightfall by now. It was not the light of sunset. It was cold and purple, an amethyst glow...and it was flickering irregularly.

Sinon grabbed the Hecate and crawled along the ground.

When she reached the entrance, she went into a prone shooting position and looked carefully up into the sky.

It was definitely nighttime. But there were no stars or moon in the sky, just a multilayered curtain of light. An aurora...and the strange sound was coming from every bit of it.

Suddenly, the aurora flickered powerfully, and a voice emerged.

"The seeds bud, sprout stems and leaves, and join ends to form a circular gate. Visitors to this land, drained of hope, preserve your solitary life. Withstand myriad trials, survive untold dangers, and to the first to reach the land revealed by the heavenly light, all shall be given."

The voice sounded like an innocent young girl's but spoke with the wisdom of a sage. Sinon didn't understand what it meant right away. The only phrases that remained in her head were "land revealed by the heavenly light" and "all shall be given."

The heavenly light had to be referring to the aurora. She gazed into the night sky again, where the purple curtains of light were arranged in concentric circles. The center seemed to be north—no, northeast. She'd have to leave to get an accurate gauge on the direction.

Sinon steeled herself to go and started to get to her feet—but she couldn't.

The rippling aurora in the sky simply vanished, like it had been turned off with a light switch. At the same time, she felt a terrible weight press upon her back. For an instant, she thought someone was actually pinning her down. But in fact, the weight was coming from the MP7, the sidearm she kept around her lower back. It had been as light as a kitten a second earlier, but now it was a lion resting on her spine.

"Urgh..."

She reached around her back, grabbed the grip of the MP7 where it stuck out of the holster, and managed to knock it loose and onto the ground. But the weight wasn't gone. It seemed her combat suit—the Sniper's Jacket, it was called—was over her Equip Weight limit.

With her right hand, she opened the ring menu and got to her equipment screen, then dragged the jacket from her mannequin to her item storage. Once the boots and muffler were off, too, she was finally light and agile again.

So this was likely what happened. In the four hours between her teleportation to this strange world at five o'clock and the mysterious announcement at nine o'clock, there was probably a grace period where she could move normally despite being encumbered. Once that period ended, Sinon's Carry Weight limit matched her low level-2 status. She was no longer able to bear the weight of her rare MP7 and the Sniper's Jacket.

Standing in her simple undergarments, Sinon looked down at the Hecate II on the floor.

She knew what would happen, but she tried to lift the barrel and stock anyway. Her gun was so immobile, it might as well have been bolted to the ground. It was an antimateriel sniper rifle, a member of the very heaviest class of weapons in *GGO*—although not as heavy as Behemoth's prized minigun. So it was no surprise that she couldn't pick it up, but it did mean she couldn't haul her favorite gun around the wilderness with her. In fact, she didn't even meet the equip requirements now, so she couldn't get down on the ground and fire it from there.

The sniper knelt on the floor of the cave and gently traced the beautiful wood stock of the Hecate.

"...Just take a little rest for now," she whispered, then tapped the gun to open a pop-up menu, and returned it to her inventory. The massive gun shone briefly, then vanished. She did the same to the MP7 with a sigh. When the virtual air filled her empty lungs, she was aware of her throat's dryness.

On sheer autopilot, she reached for the little canteen on her belt, but her hand found nothing. Like the survival knife, her canteen was gone. She'd just have to wait it out until she could replenish her water somewhere. It probably wouldn't be easy in this wilderness, but in VR, thirst was just an annoyance, not a life-and-death situation…

"Huh…?"

A nasty thought hit her. She looked to the upper left, and when she focused on the UI elements there, she gasped.

The blue TP bar was slowly decreasing. Below that, the yellow SP bar was also going down but at a slower rate than the TP bar. She intuitively knew that the bars going down had something to do with the thirst she was feeling.

T was probably short for *thirst*, she decided. It wasn't hard to figure out what would happen when that bar went all the way down. She'd collapse and die and be teleported somewhere else, leaving all her items behind. She just had to hope that if her guns were in her inventory, they couldn't be lost that way.

She stared at the blue bar again. It seemed to be falling at about 1 percent every minute. It would take a hundred minutes to deplete all the way, but she sensed that this rate would change with the environment and her physical state. It would definitely drop faster if she left the cave to search for water, expending energy.

But not doing anything wasn't an option. After the aurora vanished, the sky it left behind was full of stars, with no sign of any rain in the next hundred minutes. If she didn't find some water, she was going to die.

But there was one other problem. Sinon was dressed in nothing but underwear—top and bottom—plus a belt. The only weapon she could use was the rusty kitchen knife from the ruins. She couldn't even beat a mouse with that, much less a giant centipede.

"…No other choice, I guess," she muttered and opened her inventory.

It wasn't to take out the Hecate or MP7. She scrolled through the short list and stopped when she reached the icons for five black bags.

On the right side of the icons were their names: *Elcamino's Items*, *Suttocos's Items*, *Lian Lian's Items*, *Mishoka's Items*, and

Ichirou Masuoka's Items. If she'd beaten those players herself, she'd think nothing of using their stuff, but when she had only picked them up to save their things for safekeeping, it felt disrespectful to do it.

Still, that hesitation meant nothing to the thirst that stabbed at her throat. She checked each bag in turn, looking for weapons or armor that a level-2 character could use. The other players she'd seen here from *GGO* were fairly experienced, so their loot more than likely had requirements too high for her. But maybe one of those five played an extreme AGI build…

Thankfully, the player named Suttocos matched Sinon's hopes. In his bag was a weapon called a Bellatrix SL2 and Weasel Suit armor. She could equip them both and just barely stay below her Equip Weight limit.

After dropping the two icons onto her equipment mannequin, a long, thin laser gun appeared on the left side of her belt, and a yellowish-brown combat suit covered her body. The Bellatrix was an optical gun, which wasn't her style, and the Weasel Suit had more exposure than she would have preferred, but it was better than running around in her underwear with a rusty knife. Her muffler could stay on because it weighed practically nothing.

In *GGO*, when you equipped a gun, the remaining ammo appeared in the lower right part of your vision. But this world had no such feature, so she had to pull out the laser gun and check the energy gauge it featured on its frame. It said there was 63 percent remaining. She didn't know much about the gun, so she'd have to actually shoot it to find out how much energy it lost with each use.

Sinon put the laser gun in its holster and banished the ring menu. Her thirst abruptly became even more apparent, and she coughed. There was still time before the TP bar ran out, but the sensation was going to become unbearable before too long. It hurt to leave the shelter she'd found, but water was the top priority now.

She glanced back at the opened treasure chest, then popped back out of the narrow cave mouth and into the arid wasteland.

And here she was now—well past ten PM.

She'd spent nearly an hour on the move after leaving the cave, but Sinon still hadn't found any water. Her TP bar was under 20 percent, and the feeling of thirst was excruciating. If there wasn't any water around the rocky outcropping she was heading for, that would probably be where she died. She wanted to believe she'd just resurrect somewhere else in the world, but the phrase "preserve your solitary life" from the mysterious message stuck in her head. If a player got only one life, then maybe resurrecting didn't work after the grace period. If she died here, would she drop all her items and get sent back to *GGO*? Would she lose her entire character and all its data?

There were three major mistakes in judgment Sinon had made that had put her in this perilous situation. The first was trying to be nice and picking up the items from the centipedes' victims for them. The second was not logging out immediately after she'd found the cave and, instead, falling asleep inside it. The third was leaving the cave and heading farther into the wilderness, rather than returning toward the ruined city.

It occurred to her now that if she had searched the homes of the city carefully, there would probably have been a well or something of that nature. It had to be an intended part of the game design that players would replenish their water at the ruins and venture outward from there to explore; that was why there was no water outside. But her TP bar was already below halfway by the time she realized this, so she couldn't turn back and return to the city.

If there wasn't any water at the rocks ahead…No. She had to believe it would be there.

She didn't want to run into any monsters just before the end, so she watched the darkness very closely as she ran. She'd gained something called the Night Vision skill a while back, which gave her slightly better vision, but she couldn't see into the shadows by starlight alone. She gave any big rocks that might hide scorpions a wide berth and moved as quietly as possible.

The big rock formation's exterior was covered in shrubs. It was only a hundred yards away at this point.

That was when Sinon picked up some very important information, visually and aurally. She shrank back and ducked.

What she *saw* was a small, flickering light at the base of the rocks. The starlight was reflecting off something. Out in this desert, it couldn't be metal or glass. It had to be water.

And what she *heard* was a roar like thunder. The booming bass sound couldn't come from a lizard or rat. In typical VRMMO terms, only a large predator—often some kind of field boss—made that kind of sound.

Sinon's instinct was to grab the shoulder strap of the Hecate II, but she touched nothing. Her usual partner was in her inventory, unable to be equipped. All she could rely on now was the Bellatrix SL2. But optical handguns were used for their lightweight nature. Would that really help her against a boss?

The TP bar, now bright red, was nearly down to 10 percent. Standing here and waffling wouldn't stop it from running out in ten minutes or so. Finding another source of water was unrealistic at this point. Her only options were to wait here and die of thirst or gamble and head for the rock.

For some reason, she remembered something she'd said to the leader of a PvP squadron that had hired her once: *Show me you at least have the guts to look down the barrel of a gun and die, even if it's "just a stupid game"!*

Smirking, Sinon straightened. If she was going to die, she'd prefer combat to dehydration.

Another ferocious roar blanketed the wasteland. Sinon drew the Bellatrix and undid the safety.

She stared at the rock a hundred yards ahead. If there would be a fight, she at least needed to see the monster first. All she could tell was that something large was moving at the base of the rock formation.

A thought striking her, she crouched again and opened her menu. Sinon tapped the MP7 in her inventory, then selected the flashlight option from a submenu and materialized that instead. She stuck the miniature light that appeared to the lower mount rail of the Bellatrix. The weight was…just low enough. She couldn't pick up a single pebble after this, but the nice thing about VRMMOs was that as long as you were under that magic number, you were as nimble as if you were holding nothing at all.

The flashlight was a high-quality part, but not to the extent of a hundred yards. Sinon crept forward with utmost care. She closed to half the distance, watching for monsters and avoiding cacti and rocks.

The stone formation felt small from far away, but now that she was closer, it was nearly the height of a ten-story building. The surface was almost vertical, but viny plants hung down here and there, and she could hear trickling water. Apparently, the water was running down the surface of the rock and creating a little spring at the base.

The instant she was certain there was water, Sinon's thirst assaulted her senses. She felt like she was being choked, and she coughed violently. Her TP bar was at 8 percent…That meant she had eight minutes to drink or she would die.

Glancing away from the rock formation, she soon found the owner of the roaring. There was a huge, squat shadow moving counterclockwise around the base of the rock, as though protecting its territory—in fact, it was definitely doing that. She couldn't drink anything unless she dealt with the creature.

Before she gave up and made a desperate suicide attack, she thought of drawing its attention with a shot, then kiting it much farther away. Even if it didn't lose sight of her altogether, all she needed was a minute away from the rock to dunk herself in the water.

She moved even farther, nearing thirty yards. As a sniper, this was unbearably close to the target, but for people who fought with swords, like Kirito and Asuna, this was where they would start sprinting to close the gap.

What were they doing now? Studying back in the real world? Having fun leveling-up in *ALO*? She wanted to replenish her TP, find a new shelter, and log out so she could get in touch with them. If she told him everything that had happened to her, Kirito would probably be more jealous than startled. She couldn't wait to see that look on his face.

"...I'm going to survive this," she muttered, resting her torso against a sloped rock nearby and taking two-handed aim with the Bellatrix. Not only were there no bullet circles anymore, but this gun didn't come with a scope; she had to aim with the primitive sights and beads. Fortunately, optical-gun trajectory was unaffected by wind and gravity, unlike live-ammo guns, so any laser she fired would go exactly where the sights said—technically, a fraction of an inch lower.

The huge monster came around the far side of the rocky mountain, walking in a slow curve and turning its head in Sinon's direction. She could probably get its attention with a shot anywhere, but she wanted to hit a vital point to conserve the gun's energy.

Sinon would shift her left hand to hit the switch on the flashlight attachment, use three seconds of light to take aim, then fire. She exhaled, inhaled, and started to move her hand.

But she never actually turned on the light.

Dat-dat-dat-dat-daaaan! There was a quick series of bursts, and Sinon jumped on the spot. It was the sound of a live-ammo gun, and a very high caliber one at that.

Her first thought was that the players who'd been attacked by the centipedes had come back to recover their gear. But Sinon had spent over an hour traveling away from the ruins. Unless they had her bugged somehow, they couldn't possibly track her here.

The roaring of the large monster confirmed that. It was very clearly an angry roar, in contrast to the earlier howling meant to warn others of its territory. She could see bloodred damage effects spilling from its body.

There was another peal of thundering gunshots, but this time, she saw it happen: To the southeast of the rock, on Sinon's right side, a number of orange lights flickered briefly atop a small hill. A moment later, effects of the bullets hitting the creature's left flank lit up, and its bulk lurched to the side.

The effects vanished right away, but Sinon's eyes had enough light to make out the form of the monster. If one word could describe this thing, that word was *dinosaur.*

Sinon's apartment in the real world was in the Yoncho-me block of Yushima in Bunkyo Ward, adjacent to Ueno Park. When she had time to kill, she sometimes went to the art galleries and museums there. Her favorite was the National Museum of Nature and Science, which had hosted a dinosaur exhibit this summer. She wasn't crazy about dinosaurs in particular but had given it a look out of curiosity. The highlight was a full-body fossil of something called a *deinocheirus*, meaning "terrible hand." The enormous arms and claws certainly convinced her of why it was called that.

The monster protecting this rocky mountain was very similar to the *deinocheirus*. Its back rose upward like a hill, with a long neck atop it, a pointed head, and powerful arms and legs. Unlike the illustrations at the exhibit that imagined what the *deinocheirus* looked like, however, this one wasn't covered in feathers; instead, it had rough, armor-like skin. It seemed to be about sixteen feet tall and twice as long.

The dinosaur faltered with the impact of the large-caliber bullets but quickly recovered. It turned toward the hill where its attackers waited, pawed at the ground with its specialized front legs, then charged. With each footfall from its five-ton body, Sinon could feel the vibration in the earth around her feet.

The front slope of the hill formed a rather steep little cliff, and even a dinosaur would have trouble running right up. The players ought to be shooting it a third and fourth time, but now the hilltop was silent, for some reason. Who was attacking the beast anyway? If it wasn't Suttocos and his friends coming after Sinon for their gear, was it another group of *GGO* players who had ventured out farther? But why did all the guns sound like the exact same type?

To Sinon's amazement, the dinosaur maintained its powerful momentum and slammed its heavy head against the cliffside. That attack rumbled even harder. Cracks spread outward from the impact point.

The dinosaur then backed away, its head lowered, and tensed to charge again. At last, a third round of gunfire sent a series of red eruptions running across the dinosaur's raised spine. This time, however, it did not falter; apparently, the protuberances on its back gave it higher defense there.

"*Goaaaah!*" the dinosaur bellowed, and it bounded forward on its tree-trunk legs. It slammed into the same spot on the cliff with another headbutt. The cracks reached the top of the hillside, and clumps of dried earth fell downward.

Sinon thought she heard faint screams, and she squinted for a better look.

Along with the earth, a figure also tumbled down the side of the hill, which was about thirty feet tall. One of the people atop the lip of the cliff lost their balance as it gave way beneath them.

"……Good grief."

She was so exasperated by this display of amateurism that she forgot about the pain in her throat and leaped out of her hiding spot. She didn't know who the attackers were, but working with them was her best chance at eliminating the dinosaur and getting some water to drink. She thought about sneaking over to the spring while the battle raged on, but she hated the thought of being targeted by the dinosaur and attracting the anger of the attackers as well.

Sinon gripped the Bellatrix with both hands as she rushed toward the cliff from the south. The fallen player was trapped under rocks and couldn't get up. A fourth set of shots rang out from the hilltop, but the number of bullets was fewer. The dinosaur was unconcerned, and it lifted its front leg, threatening the fallen player with its deadly claws.

"Over here!" Sinon shouted, turning on her flashlight. The bright light pierced the darkness and struck the dinosaur's head. It briefly stopped with confusion, and she used that chance to shoot the Bellatrix in its yellow eye.

There was a comparatively weak *pshu!* sound, and a pale-green beam of light shot forth, penetrating the dinosaur's right eye.

"*Gyaooooo!!*" it shrieked. The beast smashed into the cliffside, having lost its balance thrashing about. More of the cliffside crumbled, and large amounts of dirt and rock tumbled downward. Above its head, which was similar to both a crocodile's and a bird's, a red ring cursor appeared, but she didn't have time to stand there and read.

She lowered her gun and turned off the light, then rushed to the fallen player, pushing hard against the large boulder trapping the player's leg beneath it.

"Get up!" she shouted, offering her hand—and then her eyes widened.

The collapsed figure wasn't a human. In a broader sense, you could call him humanoid, but at the very least, she had *never* seen an avatar like this in *GGO*.

The figure had a squat body covered in brown feathers, with the head of a bird of prey.

In other words, a birdman.

He reminded Sinon of the harpy-type monsters from *ALO*, but he was more birdlike in this case. His body was covered in armor made of cloth and leather, and he held a simple rifle in his hand. This couldn't be a player or a monster, but an NPC.

Sinon reversed course and thrust her hand out again. Even if his appearance was 70 percent bird, she would surely find common understanding with a fellow shooter (even if she had no evidence to back up the assertion).

It wasn't clear if the birdman understood her, but his hawklike eyes blinked once, and then he grasped Sinon's outstretched hand. She pulled him to his feet and saw that she was about two inches taller.

"Can you run?!" she asked.

But the birdman answered her in a language she couldn't begin to comprehend.

"ℵℵℵℵ."

She had no idea what he said, but there was no time to figure that out now. The dinosaur was shaking vigorously, trying to throw off all the cliffside earth that had landed on top of it.

"This way!" Sinon shouted and began to run for the rear side of the hill. The birdman followed her on naked feet that looked like an ostrich's. There was red light streaming from his left leg, but the damage didn't seem too serious.

The hill was circular in shape, about a hundred feet in diameter and fifty feet tall. There had to be a path on the other side that the birdmen had used to reach the top of the cliff. Or maybe they flew...But no, that couldn't be right. Their wings had atrophied—or perhaps evolved—into arms. The feathers from shoulder to elbow were more ornamental than anything and certainly not designed for actual flight.

As they ran, her new companion abruptly shouted, "ℵℵℵ!"

She spun around and saw him pointing at the cliff with a clawed hand. She couldn't see it very well in the dark, but she could tell there was something like a ladder there. Sinon turned as hard to the left as she could with her momentum and leaped onto the ladder. This wasn't just some rope ladder thrown down temporarily but a fixed feature that had been pounded into the rock surface with stakes. That must have meant the birdmen didn't coincidentally decide to attack that dinosaur tonight but had tried picking it off many times from the top of the hill.

Sinon hurried up the ladder as fast as she could go. The Bellatrix was back in its holster, so if the birdman tried to attack her from below, her ability to return fire would be delayed, but she didn't think he would betray her now.

Sure enough, she was able to climb the entire fifty feet of ladder without interruption. At the top of the hill was only a small selection of shrubs, with the rest being rock and sand. She'd hoped for a little bit of water but saw nothing. Her TP bar was down to 4 percent.

Thinking about it brought the sensation of thirst back with a terrible vengeance, sending Sinon to her knees. A few seconds later, the birdman reached the top of the hill, so she asked him, "Do you have any water...?"

But the birdman just blinked at her, confused. She glanced at his body and saw only two tool bags on his belt and no canteen. If he was an NPC, he wouldn't have a virtual inventory, so whatever she could see was everything he held.

So in the next four minutes—make that three and change now—she had to defeat the dinosaur and get back to the spring at the base of that mountain, or else she would die.

And I refuse to die.

Sinon summoned all her willpower to get back to her feet, then tottered into a run toward the west side of the rocky mountain. Within moments, she saw a number of silhouettes (birdhouettes?) along the cliffside. They were aiming their rifles at the base of the cliff and had their backs to her. It seemed they were going to open fire on the dinosaur for a fifth time.

But from what Sinon could see of the dinosaur's HP bar, it was still at nearly 80 percent. Their rounds of gunfire hadn't even taken off 10 percent each time. If they stayed up here at the top of the hill, the dinosaur couldn't attack directly, but the only target they could hit was the thick hide of its back. It wasn't doing a lot of damage. And based on the size of the sacks on their belts, they weren't flush with ammo, either.

"Wait!" she shouted, causing the line of birdmen to flinch. The feathers around their necks stood on end. They whipped around, pointing their guns at Sinon.

"אאא?!"

"אאאאא!!"

She raised her hands on sheer instinct and tried to argue her cause. "I'm not your enemy! I want to help you beat that dinosaur!"

"אאא!!" shouted a larger individual who stood a head taller than the rest. His rifle was steady on her. Nothing she could say was going to get through to them.

Her TP bar was at 3 percent.

I guess this is as far as I get, she lamented.

Then an impact almost as powerful as an explosion slammed the entire hill. The dinosaur had struck the cliff with another headbutt. The lip of the cliff crumbled spectacularly, and the birdmen leaped back from it, crying with dismay. The dinosaur's roar set the night air on edge.

That sound was enough to bring back Sinon's will to fight, just as it was running out.

She could wallow in despair once she died. As long as there was a single pixel left on her TP bar, she would fight to survive. She just had to make her intentions known to the birdmen and get their help to beat the dinosaur. There had to be a way to do that.

What would Kirito do in a situation like this? He probably wouldn't rely on words. He always used action—whipping everyone into battle through the sheer brilliance of his sword and the willpower contained within it. Sinon had no sword, but she did have a partner. And she was the only thing Sinon could rely on here.

She opened her ring menu and quickly moved to the STORAGE icon. In the list there, she selected the name of the gun she'd stored hours ago and brought it back into the world.

The moment the gigantic antimateriel rifle appeared atop her window, the birdmen screeched in alarm. Their guns were more like the old-fashioned muskets that matched the bullets she'd found in the cave—in no way comparable to her Hecate II, a high-precision weapon created with modern production technology. Of course, it was strange that the birdmen could use guns at all, but this was her chance to get them on her side, while they were impressed.

"You and you! Support the barrel from each side!" Sinon commanded, pointing to the largest one, who seemed to be their leader, and the one standing next to him. They tilted their heads in puzzlement. The gesture was so distinctly birdlike that she nearly laughed, but she held it in.

"Hurry!" she tried again. "We have to shoot while the dinosaur is stunned by the headbutt!"

But the birdmen did not react. It seemed they weren't going to respond to words in any way. There were android NPCs in *GGO* that spoke a mysterious language, too, but once you got a language conversion chip during a quest, they would sound Japanese again. There was probably a similar thing she needed to do to be able to speak to the birdmen, but there was no time for quests right now.

"Please, you just have to hold it up!" she begged a third time. That was when a smaller figure leaped in from behind—the first birdman, who she had saved from the rubble. He gave his right shoulder to the middle of the barrel. Instantly, the support her player window was giving the gun vanished, and the massive weight of the gun pressed onto the birdman's shoulder.

He squawked with exertion, and Sinon hurriedly reached out to the gun, grabbing the wooden grip with one hand and supporting the body with the other. But even with two of them, the best they could do was keep it off the ground. They couldn't carry it to the edge of the cliff like this.

Her TP bar was at 2 percent.

"Urgh…Grrrgh…!"

Grunting and heaving, Sinon tried to push the rifle forward, despite its being well over her Carry Weight limit. To the right of her HP bar, there was an icon like a red paperweight that was flashing rapidly. A small window appeared before her eyes, saying *Physique skill gained. Proficiency has risen to 1*, but she didn't care.

The birdman holding up the barrel was doing his best to keep it raised, but his body was slowly sinking with the weight. With each struggling moment, more fine feathers came loose from his shoulder, until this began to create damage effects on his skin.

Sinon's efforts were reaching their limit, and she was just about to fall to her knees—

—when a large hand grabbed the barrel close to its end.

The blinking of the paperweight icon slowed down. She looked up and, for a brief moment, met the eyes of the leader of the flock.

"אא!" he shouted, then lifted the barrel and rested it on his left shoulder. That didn't lessen the load until it was under her Carry Weight limit, but she felt like they might be able to transport it now.

The three of them proceeded forward unsteadily and moved the massive rifle to the edge of the cliff. She wanted to deploy the Hecate's bipod to rest it on the ground, but that wouldn't give her the right angle to aim at the dinosaur all the way at the bottom of the cliff.

"Crouch down and keep holding it up!" she instructed, knowing the birdmen weren't going to understand her. But they quickly knelt, and Sinon stuck her cheek to the side of the Hecate and tilted the muzzle downward with all her strength.

But the dinosaur was already recovering from the wobbliness of its most recent collision. Its burly head was pointed in their direction, and it was backing up, preparing for its next blow. That wasn't good; if it hit the cliff now, the Hecate could tumble out of her grasp and off the side of the hill.

The dinosaur's HP bar, shaped like a combination of ring and pillar, also displayed the target's name in Japanese. It read *Sterocephalus*, which certainly sounded like a dinosaur, although she didn't know what it meant.

Regardless, the head of the *sterocephalus* was protected by thick, shell-like armor, and perhaps even the Hecate couldn't break through it. And that was assuming she could actually hit that target at all, at a time when she couldn't even lift the weapon. It was going to be nearly impossible.

So she'd have to aim for its huge torso instead, preferably the heart. But the *sterocephalus* wasn't even exposing its sides to her, much less its belly. Could she shoot its heart all the way through its back?

Her TP bar was down to 1 percent remaining. Sinon had sixty seconds left to live.

"...Firing now!" she exclaimed through a throat drier than the wasteland sands.

But before she could pull the trigger, the leader birdman supporting the muzzle lifted a hand and shouted, "ℵℵℵℵℵ!!"

The other birdmen lined up on either side of Sinon and aimed their muskets. The old-fashioned guns, which didn't have the benefit of rifling inside their barrels, could barely break the surface of the dinosaur's hide. They couldn't hit it in the heart. But with another short cry from the leader, they shot in unison.

Within each musket, the flint on the end of the hammer scraped the frizzen, creating sparks that lit the priming charge in the pan. A moment later, the gunpowder within the barrels exploded and propelled the bullets out of the muskets with a tremendous *bang!*

The spray of bullets almost entirely missed the dinosaur. Instead, they gouged out the ground around its feet, creating a huge wave of spark effects.

"*Gwoeaaah!*" roared the *sterocephalus*, standing on its rear legs and lifting its front arms high in the air. The action exposed its whitened belly, which was not covered in heavy natural armor.

This is it.

Sinon aimed through the scope at a spot she suspected was the *sterocephalus*'s heart, then hastily pulled the trigger. The blast it produced made the muskets sound like toys. Orange flames shot from the muzzle brake. Even with three people holding it, the recoil was too great, throwing Sinon and the two birdmen backward, along with the gun itself.

But Sinon was certain of what she saw. The .50 BMG round struck the center of the *sterocephalus*'s chest, creating an eruption of damage effects.

As they landed on their backs, the massive dinosaur's HP bar began to plummet. Down and down it went, from yellow to red—to zero.

She could hear the rumbling of the giant beast falling to the ground, even from atop the cliff. A new message appeared before her eyes: *Sinon's level has risen to 16.* She was momentarily stunned at the huge jump in levels—but then it occurred to her that maybe it would refill all of her gauges. Sadly, the tiny sliver of TP was not moving. She had forty—no, thirty—seconds until it was gone.

With a trembling finger, she tapped the Hecate next to her and put it back in her inventory.

In concert with that motion, the birdmen all raised their muskets high in the air and issued high-pitched shouts. The leader and the one Sinon saved got to their feet and joined in the exultation.

But there was no time to watch. No time to descend the ladder behind her, either.

Sinon got to her feet and sprinted for the cliffside. She had to banish her fear and leap off the fifty-foot hill. With her upgrade to level-16, she could probably survive an outright fall of that height, but she wasn't trying to gamble that hard. Instead, she was aiming for the toppled body of the *sterocephalus.*

Her feet landed on the relatively soft flank of the dinosaur, and she bent her knees to tumble forward on a diagonal, hoping to deflect as much of the impact as possible. Ever since Kirito had taught her that fall damage in Seed VRMMOs changed depending on if you fell or if you braced yourself for impact, she'd practiced it in *ALO.* Thanks to that, she lost only 10 percent of her HP bar, but there was only a single pixel of TP left.

She slid down the dinosaur's flank and hit the ground. Her vision clouded slightly, although she couldn't tell if that was just adrenaline or a simulated effect of such. There were about two hundred yards from here to the glimmering spring at the base of the rocky mountain. She could sprint there in about ten seconds.

Gritting her teeth, Sinon launched into motion. One, two, three steps, and she was at a full sprint...and that was when the TP bar silently depleted.

The worst feeling of dehydration yet burned her throat. The

looming rock blurred so that she was seeing double, and she closed her eyes.

I guess that's it.

She waited for death to arrive, leaving her last words for the Hecate II in her inventory:

If I lose you somehow, I'm going to do everything it takes to get you back.

The strength was draining from her body. She collapsed forward onto the ground. Gravelly sand brushed her cheek. Her avatar was disintegrating into.........

Nothing.

It wasn't disintegrating at all.

Instead, she noticed that the HP bar in the upper left corner was now decreasing. So when TP reached zero, it wasn't instant death, just the start of the damage to her HP. Her eyes shot open as she lay prone on the sand.

"You could have warned me of that first!" she grumbled.

No one answered, of course. She steadily lifted herself up. Death hadn't come for her yet, but there was no time to waste. The HP bar was decreasing fast enough that she could see it plummeting. Her new grace period was maybe a minute long at best.

Sinon's vision was still doubled, which told her that it was a visual-effect warning that she was at death's door. Struggling to her feet, she resumed running for the rock ahead. She bumped into smaller ones along the way, and by the time she crossed the two hundred yards thirty seconds later, her HP bar was under the halfway point.

There were beautiful, delicate flowers at the base of the rock, and a pristine surface of water swayed beyond them. She swore to herself that if this turned out to be a poisonous swamp, she would track down the people who created this mysterious world and pump them full of lead. She crossed the patch of flowers and knelt at the edge of the water.

Sinon had no cup, so she thrust her hands into the flickering sky of stars below. The water was shockingly cold. She lifted her hands to her lips and drank deeply, without bothering to taste first.

"Ah..."

She gasped. Then she scooped and drank again. And again. And again.

The dropping of her HP bar stopped, and the TP bar began to recover, but the rejuvenation she was feeling completely overrode any attention for small details like those. Scooping the water with her hands felt too slow, so she lowered her mouth directly to the water to slake her thirst like animals did.

She never wanted to leave this rock. She wanted to build a house and live here. Sinon drank and drank from the life-giving pool, not even noticing that her TP bar was already back to full again.

2

The returnee school that Asuna, Lisbeth, Silica, and I attended was located in a renovated public school that had previously been abandoned after two local high schools combined into one.

Due to this, the campus was surprisingly complex and contained a number of spots that, like in an RPG, you couldn't find unless you already knew they existed. The patch of green I was standing on was one of them—you had to go upstairs in the extracurricular club building, head all the way down the hall, exit through the emergency door, go down the outside stairs, then walk along the planters until you passed through a tiny gap you wouldn't notice otherwise.

This patch of grass, surrounded by the tall planters, the club building, and the library building, was a rectangle about thirty feet to a side. In the middle, where the earth was slightly raised, was a white siris tree and a sandalwood tree, side by side, surrounded by seasonal flowers. Soft grass covered the ground, and there were essentially no weeds. Someone had to be tending the space, but I'd never seen whomever it was.

Ever since I'd found the place this past spring, Asuna and I referred to it as the "secret garden" to keep its information private. Alas, Lisbeth had figured it out after that, so she and Silica visited it, too. And now there was a fifth person—actually, sixth, if you counted the unknown gardener—who knew about the garden.

This fifth person surveyed the space and said in a distinctive voice, "Well, well, this sure looks like a nice, tidy date spot. Ya sure ya wanted to bring me here?"

"I didn't really have a choice after that flashy entrance," I grumbled but caught myself and shook my head. "First of all, it's not a date spot. So it's perfectly fine if I show it to you."

"Awww, it's been so long. Ya don't have to be so cold, Kiri-boy. Don'tcha want a warm reunion hug?"

The small teenage girl, who wore a khaki hoodie over a dark sailor uniform, and a small day pack, held out her arms. She was only slightly shorter than Asuna and maybe an inch or so taller than Silica. She seemed to have grown quite a bit since the time I'd visited her regularly...meaning the girl who always seemed much older than I was still growing, even now.

Argo the Rat.

That was the name of the talented info dealer from back in the floating castle of Aincrad—who'd shown up in my classroom at returnee school out of nowhere just a number of minutes ago. At a school with such a distinct imbalance between boys and girls—in favor of boys—there was no way an unfamiliar girl in another school's uniform would go without notice. So I'd grabbed Argo by the arm and zipped out of the room before the other guys could crowd around. Since it was lunch period and the halls were packed with students, the only place I could go was this little green space. Once we were alone, there was a different kind of tension in the air.

I backed away from Argo's smile and outstretched hands. "I...I'll save that for the next occasion."

"You've always been a coward, Kiri-boy."

"I'm fine with that! More important...what the hell are you doing here?" I asked at last. Argo stuck her hands into the pockets of her hoodie and grinned. I couldn't help but stare at her face.

The features beneath that light-colored curly hair were the

same as those of the Rat I knew so well in Aincrad. But because of the lack of face-painted whiskers on her cheeks or because it had been two—or make that four—years since the very start of the deadly game, she seemed much more adult. In all honesty, the first time I'd met Argo in Aincrad, I couldn't be sure if she was a boy or a girl. But looking at her now, even if you subtracted the girl's uniform, there was no mistaking her feminine nature. I almost felt a little self-conscious treating her as brusquely as I typically did.

Argo apparently sensed that I was feeling a little awkward, so she came closer, wearing a teasing smile, and said, "What am I doing here? I transferred, of course."

"H-huhhh?!" I shouted, then clamped my mouth shut. In a more measured tone, I hissed, "Transferred? It's been two years since we escaped. Why now? And more important, why didn't you ever contact me? I thought for sure you were..."

I couldn't say the rest. Argo just smiled and shrugged. "You know I wouldn't kick the bucket. Besides, ya can't knock me for not gettin' in touch when I could say the same of you. With your connections, you coulda learned my contact info easily."

"......"

She was right.

In the *SAO* days, I didn't know Argo's real name or address or phone number, but I did know the character name "Argo." If I'd given that info to Seijirou Kikuoka at the Ministry of Internal Affairs and Communications' Virtual Division, he would have pulled all the information contained in that user's data for me.

But it wasn't just Argo; I didn't proactively search out *any* of the players I knew in *SAO* whose life or death was unknown to me. The group who'd survived the seventy-fifth-floor boss battle would have logged out safely, I assumed, but everyone else—like Mr. Nishida or Kibaou, Nezha, Mahocle, and so on—could be either alive or dead, as far as I knew. I didn't try to find out because I was scared. I didn't want to hear from Kikuoka's mouth, with all finality, that they hadn't come back.

For the same reason, I didn't want to find out Argo's real-life information. I started to lower my head to apologize.

But with the same speed she had back in *SAO*, Argo closed the gap and jabbed my forehead with her index and middle fingers, pushing me back up straight.

"Did I ask ya to apologize? I said we were both responsible for not gettin' in touch. You've been kickin' so much ass in *ALO* and *GGO* under your own name, I coulda reached out and made contact if I tried."

Argo let go and retreated a step. I rubbed my forehead, unsure of how to react. In the end, I just asked her straight up:

"That's just it...Why didn't you come to *ALO*? You're not the kind of person who would get freaked out by full-dive machines now, right?"

"Uh, who do you think I am?" She grimaced. Argo stuck her hands into her pockets again and rocked back and forth. "Mmm. Well, there are reasons. It's not like I didn't care about it at all. When I heard you could bring back your old *SAO* character in *ALO*, that was a big temptation. But...I knew that if I went into business as an info dealer again in *ALO*, I wouldn't have the same motivation I did back then..."

"Yeah...I guess I can understand that," I said. But the truth was that I understood it all too well.

Sword Art Online was a true alternate world created by the mad genius Akihiko Kayaba. It trapped us in a floating land of rock and steel and demanded that its players beat the game with a horrifying caveat: If you die in the game, you die in real life.

Hardly a single day went by back then that I didn't feel fear, despair, panic, or anguish. But those weren't the only things I felt in the game. There was joy in a level-up, excitement at acquiring a rare bit of loot, exultation after defeating a boss monster. They were true, heartfelt emotions unlike anything I had experienced in the games I'd played before *SAO*. As hard as it was to admit, even my main game now, *ALO*, which I truly enjoyed, didn't elicit the same level of dedication that *SAO* had...

But I brushed that momentary sentiment aside and asked, "In that case...what have you been doing the last two years, and where?"

"I've been going to school where I live, obviously."

"Oh..."

But of course. That should have been obvious. I'd been through a lot after *SAO*, as well, but for the most part, what I did boiled down to "going to school where I live."

"Where are you from? What year are you in?"

Argo thrust out her right hand and replied, "Two questions'll cost ya a thousand col."

"Oh, right..."

I reached into my uniform pocket for a thousand-col gold coin before I stopped myself. Argo just laughed.

"Nya-ha-ha-ha...I'm just kiddin'. I live in the lower left part of Kanagawa, and I'm in my last year of high school."

"Lower left," I murmured, consulting a mental map of Kanagawa Prefecture. I knew that in the southwestern part of it were the cities of Odawara, Hakone, and Atami...but the last one was actually in Shizuoka. In any case, they weren't exactly close to Tokyo. If she was in the third year of high school, that made her a year above me. Like Asuna and Liz, she'd be graduating in the latter half of the year.

"...Why would you transfer here *now*?"

"Mmm." Argo grunted, then shrugged and said, "Ah, might as well." She reached for the little day pack she was wearing. Her fingers dexterously found the pocket on the back without looking, and she pulled out a rectangular case. It was made of yellow leather, and she removed a gray card from it that she handed to me.

I took the item, which I saw was actually a business card. My eyes were drawn to the name printed in the middle of its face.

"Tomo...Hosaka. That's your real name?"

"Sorry, it doesn't sound like it'd be my name, huh?"

"Erm, I didn't mean it like that...I was just surprised that you'd tell me your real name that easily..."

"I'm transferring to this school. It's not like I can hide it forever." Argo, aka Tomo Hosaka, pouted.

I looked back at the business card. Right beneath her name was an e-mail address and phone number. On the upper left was her title. To my surprise, it said MMO TODAY, WRITER/RESEARCHER.

"Wait, really?!" I exclaimed.

That reaction alone told her what I had spotted on the card. She nodded and said, "Yep."

"So you're a writer for MMO Today...Meaning I might have already read several articles you've written without realizing it...?"

"Probably."

"But isn't MMO Today centered around news about The Seed? Can you write articles if you're not playing the games?"

"I'm not covering individual games. I'm more focused on overall news of The Seed Nexus and the hardware end, I guess. Sometimes I'll whip up a character and do a quick dive, but as soon as my research is done, I delete 'em."

"Ohhh..."

I exhaled and looked over Argo's face again. It wasn't particularly shocking that she was one year older than I, but hearing that she was a writer for MMO Today, the biggest source of news on the world of VRMMOs, made me feel like the gap between us was that much larger. I didn't even have a part-time job.

"...I guess...I have to treat you with more respect...From now on, I'll call you Miss Hosaka..."

"Knock it off! Just be normal," Argo snapped quite seriously. She jutted her chin at me accusingly and said, "Well? You're gonna make me introduce myself and won't do me the same courtesy?"

"Huh? Oh, right..."

At long last, I realized I hadn't actually told her *my* real name. It felt awkward to do it now, after all this time, but I didn't have a business card to do the talking for me.

"Well, uh...my real name is Kazuto Kirigaya. It's good to see you again."

"Yep. Likewise," she said, grinning, and stuck out her right hand. Her palm was vertical this time, making it clear she was asking for a handshake, not payment. I hesitantly reached out and grabbed it.

She squeezed firmly. Through her skin, I felt a pulse that didn't belong to me.

"...You're alive," I said, the words I couldn't bring myself to say earlier.

Argo smiled at me again, though the nuances of its warmth were slightly different this time. "It's thanks to you, Kiri-boy. The truth is, I didn't see myself lasting until the hundredth floor. If you hadn't beaten it on the seventy-fifth, I'd have prob'ly kicked the bucket somewhere before then."

"It wasn't just me..."

That was all I could say. There was a sudden wrenching feeling in my chest. And it was true—I only defeated Heathcliff, aka Akihiko Kayaba, because of the support, encouragement, and guidance of many players. That included Argo, of course.

I'm so glad she survived, I thought, savoring the emotion, before I let go of her hand. I inhaled the forest-scented air, then exhaled, ridding myself of all those lingering feelings. Then I got back on topic.

"So...what's the relation between you transferring to this school and your writing position with MMO Today?"

"Ahhh, that..."

But Argo didn't say another word. She glanced toward the gap between the planters, which was the only way in or out of the secret garden. I started to hear some quick, sprightly footsteps.

A few seconds later, Asuna burst into the green space, holding her phone in one hand. I'd sent her a text while we were on the way over here. Asuna came to a stop on the grass, looked at me first, then at Argo next to me.

"...No way..."

Her hazel-brown eyes glittered with the light trickling through the leaves overhead. Argo blinked, too, then lifted her hand and made a waving motion.

"Hiya. How ya been, A-cha—?"

But she couldn't finish her question. Asuna charged with such speed that she seemed to be possessed by her old identity, the Flash of *SAO*, and she wrapped the smaller woman in a tremendous hug. Her phone slipped out of her right hand in the process, and I just barely managed to catch it before it hit the ground.

Asuna buried her face in Argo's shoulder and murmured, "I knew...I *knew* I would see you again one day."

"...Sorry I haven't been in touch for a while, A-chan," she whispered, patting the back of the other girl's blouse. Once they separated, Asuna stared her in the face, then said the exact same thing I had several minutes earlier.

"So, um...what exactly are you doing here, Argo?"

Lunch period at returnee school lasted from 12:40 to 1:30. Fifty minutes was a long lunch for a high school, but we didn't have enough time to sit around and reminisce. Plus, when you were a growing teenager, skipping lunch was not an option if you wanted to survive the day.

So the message I sent to Asuna on the way over was GET THREE PORTIONS OF SOMETHING FROM CAFETERIA, COME TO SECRET GARDEN. Asuna brought three baguette sandwiches. One of them was Camembert, ham, and arugula. The second was cream cheese, smoked salmon, and tomato. The last was shrimp, avocado, and basil. We set down a lightweight polyethylene sheet at the foot of the sandalwood tree, and Asuna gave Argo the first choice of sandwiches.

"Pick whichever one you like, Argo. This is on me."

"Ah, geez, I can't do that," she protested, but Asuna shoved the three sandwiches toward her face with a smile.

"Yes, you can. Remember how you helped us with the quest when we were buying the house in the forest on the twenty-second floor? I'm paying you back for that!"

"...Ahhh, right, that *did* happen," Argo said, her eyes narrowing as she reminisced. "All right, I'll accept yer gift. I think I'll take...this one."

With a grin, she took the smoked salmon baguette. Asuna turned to look at me and asked which one I wanted. Out of the two, I figured she would want the avocado, so I told her, "Ham and cheese!"

Despite being two years since we were released from *SAO*—and living together with Asuna for only two weeks in that world—I couldn't get past the habits from sharing an inventory back then. And I had developed a bad one: Whenever Asuna paid for something for the both of us, I often forgot to pay her back. I only realized it this time after I'd taken the sandwich, and I quickly pulled out my phone. Asuna had bought us three iced teas, too, so I totaled the cost of three portions, divided by two, and input that into the payment app so Asuna's device could read the code it displayed. It was even easier to send personal payments using an Augma, but in my panic, I left that in my bag back in the classroom.

At that very moment, I froze, phone in one hand and baguette in the other, and gasped, "Oh…!!"

We were supposed to be using this lunch period to meet with Liz and Silica in the cafeteria to talk about the anomaly that had shaken The Seed Nexus to its core yesterday. On top of that, Suguha and Sinon were supposed to take part using Augmas from their high schools in Ohmiya and Ueno. All of them were waiting for me and Asuna to join them right now.

Argo gave me an odd look, but Asuna just rolled her eyes and said, "So you *did* forget. Don't worry—I got in touch with everyone and asked them to postpone the meeting until after school."

"Oh…th-thanks," I said sheepishly.

Argo ducked her head, too, and said, "Did ya have plans already? Sorry for messin' that up."

"It's fine. I knew that lunch break was going to be way too short for what we need to do, anyway," Asuna explained, passing us the cups of iced tea. "Come on—let's eat. I'm starving."

I wasn't about to argue with that suggestion. I peeled back the paper and bit down on the end of the sandwich where the insides jutted out. A local ran the meal stand in the cafeteria, so while the food was premade, the baguette crust was fragrant and the veggies were fresh. I ate a few bites in silence, then washed them down with some iced tea.

Argo finished half of hers in no time, looking thoroughly satisfied. "This ain't your average cafeteria food. I made the right choice comin' here."

"Pretty much everything on the cafeteria menu is good. But… aside from that," I said, clearing my throat and returning to the suspended topic of conversation, "you gotta tell us why you decided to transfer now of all moments."

"The timing's not that weird, ya know. This school splits its admission period into early and late periods, and this is the entrance date for the late admissions."

"What, really? Then…they should have just made it a two-semester system, rather than a trimester…"

"Then ya wouldn't have winter vacation."

"Okay, never mind, then," I replied immediately.

Asuna giggled and explained, "This school only developed an admissions system this August. So it wasn't in time for the end of summer vacation, and they had to set it up for the end of September instead. That makes Argo transfer student number one. Also, they say you don't have to be a former *SAO* player to transfer in."

"Really…? But is any student at a normal school actually going to want to come to this place? I feel like society treats this like its own unique, isolated thing…"

"Yes, but because it's a specialty school, lots of the curricula are practical in nature, right? You can select the units you really want to learn about…And since the media's been reporting on the various unique qualities of the school, more people are getting interested. There was a transfer student in my class, too, and they said the same thing."

"Uh-huh…So Argo's here for the same…," I said before coming to a realization.

The anomaly we were supposed to talk about with the others—the forced conversion of players from every Seed VRMMO into the mysterious *Unital Ring*—started yesterday, September 27th.

And Argo, who was writing articles about The Seed Nexus for MMO Today, transferred here out of nowhere on September 28th.

Was that really a coincidence? Argo claimed it was the first day of school for the later admissions, but that couldn't be the only reason.

"Argo, are you actually here because of *Unital*—?"

She cut me off by pressing her index finger against my lips.

"Don't be in such a rush, Kiri-boy. I'll give ya a proper explanation, but I don't have enough time for it now. Mind if I join you for that after-school meeting?"

"Wh...what?"

Asuna and I shared stunned looks.

In the *SAO* days, Argo had contributed much to our advancement through the deadly game, thanks to her business as an info dealer. But around the middle floors, she was focused on behind-the-scenes matters, and even I hardly saw her after that point. Silica and Liz might have known her name, but they probably never bought or sold her information, and Leafa and Sinon would have no point of reference for her whatsoever.

But thinking back on it, Liz and Silica had only met Leafa a year and a half ago, and Sinon just nine months before. But now they were so close, it was like they'd been friends for years. Argo had a chance to fit in, too. Asuna and I nodded and turned back to Argo.

"That's fine. But...just...don't say anything weird, okay?"

"Whaddaya mean, 'weird'?"

"I'm counting on your good judgment in that regard," I said in all seriousness and resumed eating my baguette. Argo would make good friends with the others, I told myself, and tried not to listen to the note of foreboding in the back of my mind.

* * *

At three thirty, after the end of our last short homeroom period, I quickly left the class for the computer lab, which was on the northern end of the third floor of Building Two.

It was called a "lab" because the place had once held classes on information technology when it was a public school; there wasn't actually some giant mainframe there. And most of the desktop PCs that had been there were removed by now, so the room definitely didn't live up to its name.

As students of the school's mechatronics course, two other boys and I formed a research team and were officially borrowing the computer lab from the school. Each of us had a key to the door, but the other two were going to Akihabara to look for parts today, which made it a convenient place for our meeting.

I rushed down the connecting hallway between the buildings, then climbed the stairs to the third floor. I assumed I'd be first there, but Lisbeth, aka Rika Shinozaki, was already waiting outside the room.

"You're late!" Liz shouted as soon as she saw me.

I knifed my hand and dipped my head in apology. "No way. You're just early! I sprinted here as soon as my homeroom let out..."

"Well, my homeroom teacher is away on an assignment, so I didn't have any homeroom. What else am I supposed to do?"

"Waste some time in your class before you come over..."

"I decided to walk slowly, so I would arrive at the right time!"

We bickered the same way we did so often in *ALO*, but here at school, I was in my second year, while Liz was a third-year student, so I felt the tiniest bit submissive. Klein and Agil were much older, and I could speak with them as equals, so this had something to do with the structural power of school years. If they made a Seed game set in a gigantic school, would it be popular? Maybe there already was one.

"Why are you spacing out? C'mon, open the door already."

Liz smacked me on the back amicably, and I returned to my

senses. There was a key with a faded plastic tag in my pocket. I took it out and stuck it into the keyhole. The cranky old cylinder lock turned. I pulled open the sliding door, held my hand to my chest, and bowed.

"After you, Mistress Lisbeth."

"Thank you, manservant," she said smugly, and I followed her into the computer lab. We tried to vacuum it as often as possible, but there was no escaping that particular smell of old classrooms. The afternoon sun blazed through the white curtains, creating a strong enough contrast of light that we didn't need to hit the switch.

"Ooh, nice. I really like the atmosphere in here," commented Liz, who had never been to the lab before. I was so used to it that it didn't elicit any emotions in me. If it were a wooden building, then maybe there would be a photogenic quality to it, but Building Two wasn't that old. The walls were slightly cracked concrete, the floors were faded linoleum, and the desks were cheap melamine surfaces. But Liz crossed the room, looking at everything with great curiosity, and turned back to me with an enigmatic smile when she reached the window.

"Doesn't this seem like a scene from an anime set at a school? After class, at the older school building, where a boy and girl are alone together..."

I leaned backward, slightly freaked by her implications.

She jabbed a finger at me and finished, "...having a crazy battle with psychic powers!"

"A battle, huh...?" I replied, exasperated.

Liz lowered her hand and cackled. "What else would we do?"

"Nothing at all. Anyway...what's taking everyone else so long?" I wondered, right as the door slid open again.

"Thanks for waiting." "Sorry about the delay!"

That was Asuna and Silica, coming in together. And behind them...no third person.

Did Argo ask us to let her join the meeting and then back out of it? I reached for my phone to get in touch with her, then remembered that we hadn't traded information. The image of Argo the

Rat in the secret garden just two hours ago was already fading into dappled sunlight in my mind. As though Asuna and I had witnessed an illusion…

"Hiya!" said a very casual voice, and Argo herself trotted through the open doorway.

I nearly fell onto the floor. Asuna waved at her and smiled, but Liz and Silica were dumbfounded.

Argo, still dressed in her hoodie, noticed them and gave a little bow, then turned to me and said, "Hey, introduce me already."

"Oh, right…Uh, Liz, Silica, this is Argo. As of today, she's a transfer student at the school. She's an *SAO* survivor like us, and back in Aincrad—"

Argo cut in smoothly and continued, "Back in Aincrad, I was Kiri-boy's *special friend*."

"Kiri-boy?!" cried Liz.

"Special friend?!" cried Silica.

I performed a slide dash, rushing to Argo's side, where I successfully withstood the urge to yank her around by the hood of her jacket. Instead, I hissed, "What did I tell you about not saying anything weird?!"

"Whaddaya mean? It's the truth."

"How is that the truth?! We weren't anything other than salesperson and customer, and you know it!"

"Why, what a cold thing to say. After all the times I offered ya preferential treatment…"

Asuna had heard enough of the bickering and snipped, "Can we leave it at that and get down to business? We can introduce Argo during the meeting. Otherwise we'll have to do it again for Suguha and Shino-non."

"Oh, r-right…Good point," I said, seeing the stunned looks on Liz's and Silica's faces. "I'll explain who she is very soon, so why don't we prep for the meeting now?"

"Are you all right? You sort of tripped over your words there," noted Silica, fixing me with a piercing gaze. I quickly backed away and made a beeline for my school bag.

* * *

The desks in the computer lab weren't classroom desks but long desks for seating three people. We pushed two together in the center of the room to make an impromptu meeting table. Asuna and Argo sat on the left side of the desk, Liz and Silica lined up on the right, and I sat at the end, closest to the door.

All of us wore Augmas—Argo's was painted mustard yellow, with a little rat symbol on the battery holder in the back. Once they were all booted up, a little fairy-sized Yui appeared over the desk.

"Papa, Mama, Liz, Silica! Hello!" she said in a cute little voice. Then she noticed Argo. "And this must be…"

"Oh, er, I'm going to explain in a minute, as soon as we start the—," I started to say, but Yui just blinked once and then grinned.

"Argo! You were very helpful to Papa and Mama in *SAO*. My name is Yui," she said, bowing.

Argo's mouth just hung open. "Uhhh…how did you know I was Argo…?"

"Your biometrics are a ninety-nine percent match to your *SAO* avatar data!"

"But…I grew a fair bit the last two years…"

"I run a growth simulation during my identification process!" Yui chirped, at which point Argo finally seemed to understand that Yui was an AI, not an actual child.

After three seconds of silence, she reached a hand over the desk. "W-well, it's nice to be working with you."

"Yes, likewise!"

Yui grabbed Argo's thumb with her tiny hands. It occurred to me that Yui's information-collection abilities, which were far beyond those of any organic human being, had to be a source of envy for Argo, who was still doing a kind of info-dealer job in the real world. As Yui returned to the center of the table, I made a mental note to keep an eye on her and make sure she didn't get recruited for any fishy side jobs.

Yui spread her hands and said, "Now I'll connect to Sinon and Leafa!"

There was a visual effect like whitish sparks in the air, and Sinon and Suguha appeared on the window end of the table. They were both wearing their school uniforms and sat in chairs with different designs.

This was the first time trying out Yui's AR meeting system, but the realism of the experience was stunning; it was like there were two other people physically present in the room with us. They were just as shocked, and they looked around the computer lab with amazement.

"...Wow...so this is returnee school...," murmured Sinon, who started to get up from her chair, but I held out my hands to stop her.

"No, don't move! What you're seeing is being overwritten by the Augma, so if you move around, you'll bump into stuff and fall over."

"Oh...right. By the way, I'm in the language lab. So if some other student comes in, they'll see me just sitting by myself, talking to nothing, right?" Sinon asked.

Yui enthusiastically confirmed this, and Suguha made a face. "Ugh, I'm connecting from the nurse's office. Someone's sure to come by..."

"What about your club, Sugu?" I asked.

The kendo team member stuck out her tongue. "I took time off today."

"Wait, really? Are you sure? What if the third-years take it out on you?"

"I'll be just fine, thank you very much! Besides, the third-years graduated from the club after nationals in August, so I'm the vice-captain now."

"Wait, really? You should have said so! We haven't done any celebrations for you."

"Being made vice-captain isn't worth making a fuss over. But if I go far in the newcomer competition in November, I'll demand a major party!"

We were just having a sibling chat in the midst of this important meeting. But Silica looked surprised and asked Suguha, "If you're the vice-captain, then is there someone better than you in the club?"

"Oh, you bet. I win some and lose some in practice, but I kind of follow my own individual style...You want an orthodox person to be your team captain."

I was starting to worry about her getting bullied again, but the kendo club wouldn't choose an unpopular member to be vice-captain. Nationals had happened in early August, when I was still in the hospital, so I hadn't been able to go cheer her on. The newcomer competition for first- and second-years after the seniors left was coming up, so I definitely needed to be there for it.

"Anyway," I said, "let's not waste any more time. First of all, I want to introduce her—er, our guest, I mean."

I pointed to Argo, who rose from her seat and bowed.

"This is a new transfer student at returnee school as of today, Tomo Hosaka...But in *SAO*, she was the info dealer known as Argo the Rat."

Immediately, Liz and Silica said in unison, "Ohhh! From the strategy guides!" Sinon and Suguha looked at them suspiciously, muttering "Strategy guides?" Argo herself giggled nervously and stood up again so she could give handshakes to the four people aside from me, Asuna, and Yui—although in the case of the two remote partners, they had to mimic shaking hands.

Of course, it also occurred to me that this was only worsening the imbalance of boys and girls on the team. There were tons of male VRMMO players at this school, so if we wanted to recruit more to the group, it would have been easy, but I just never really felt like it. That was probably because I'd already met the greatest friend I could ever have after two years in the Underworld. I didn't think I'd ever have another guy friend my age I'd reach such a close understanding with, and I didn't really want to. When he died in battle, a part of me died with him. That was a scar that would never heal for the rest of my life, most likely.

I took a deep breath of wax-scented air, stifling the sharp pain in my chest, and stated, "Now that introductions are over, let's get down to business. The first thing I want to know is the state of non-*ALO* players...You got converted into *Unital Ring* from *GGO*, too, didn't you, Sinon?"

"Yep," she agreed, drawing everyone's attention.

"And just to confirm, you know that your avatar stays in the virtual space after you log out, right? Are you in a safe location?"

"Well...I think I'm safe. The birdmen are protecting me."

Everyone, including me, looked puzzled at that. Sinon just shrugged, as if to say she didn't get it, either.

3

The bus heading to the north gate of Kichijoji Station was surprisingly empty. Asuna sat close to the exit, rested her school bag on her knees, and exhaled.

The warmth of the unexpected reunion with Argo still buzzed in her chest. But at the same time, there was something discordant about the day. That feeling was coming from her meeting with the other transfer student, Shikimi Kamura.

There hadn't been any hostility from Shikimi, not at all. They'd talked for just a few minutes, and she'd been completely relaxed the entire time. The reason she'd come over to say hello, despite being in the classroom next door, was because, according to her, they'd met at a party within the electronics manufacturing industry years and years ago. Asuna didn't remember her, but Shikimi Kamura was apparently the daughter of the founder of Kamura, the makers of the Augma and rival to RCT Progress.

But it wasn't Shikimi's background that distressed Asuna's subconscious so much.

It was her uniform. She was wearing the high school uniform of Eterna Girls' Academy, a unified twelve-year school in Minato Ward—the school that Asuna had attended before she'd become prisoner to *Sword Art Online.*

Asuna had only attended through middle school, but she did not remember ever knowing a student in her year with the family name of Kamura. It was a distinctive name, and Shikimi had a striking appearance, so she couldn't possibly have missed seeing her during all three years of school.

That meant Shikimi had come to the high school of Eterna Girls' Academy from somewhere else and, half a year before graduation, transferred to the returnee school instead.

Asuna asked if that was going to have a negative effect on her exams, but Shikimi was planning to go to college overseas and had already received a diploma from the International Baccalaureate and an official SAT score report. She'd heard that American colleges valued the essay portion just as much as the score, which helped explain the decision to come to the returnee school, where there was a greater degree of freedom for scholastic pursuits. But it still seemed like an extreme decision, and it was hard for Asuna to shake the unpleasant idea that Shikimi viewed the school like a special subsidy to take advantage of.

That impression was probably coming from the uniform Shikimi was wearing. If the *SAO* Incident hadn't happened, Asuna might have been wearing that gray blazer, too. Eterna's middle school had a featureless jumper dress for a uniform, so the blazer jackets the high schoolers wore, with their navy-blue collars, looked sharp by comparison. Her mother had told her to take exams for other high schools anyway, so she might not have had the chance to wear it, but it was hard not to think negative thoughts when faced with it once again.

Asuna didn't have a complex about attending her current school, and she didn't harbor any secret wishes to redo her life from four years ago. But looking at Shikimi Kamura in that uniform, it was like…It was like she was looking at herself as a student at Eterna Girls' Academy had she never been trapped in *SAO*…

"…This is stupid," she muttered, closing her eyes. There were nine more bus stops until Kichijoji Station. She was likely to stay up all night again tonight, so she had to find her sleep where she could.

Asuna rested her head against the wall of the bus, but sleep would not visit her. In the back of her mind, she couldn't shake the image of Shikimi's perfectly pristine features, a clever beauty that, for some reason, stirred up a faint anxiety in Asuna.

Asuna had no complaints with her life. She loved and trusted Kazuto and Yui with all her heart, and she'd met the best possible friends in Rika, Keiko, Shino, and Suguha. No matter what Shikimi, with her perfectly unblemished record, might think of her, Asuna knew that she was perfectly happy.

But the fact that I have to tell myself that is a sign I'm shaken by this.

Asuna let out a long, slow breath and decided to think only about what pleasures awaited her.

The forced conversion to the mysterious VRMMO *Unital Ring* had brought great confusion and chaos to The Seed Nexus, but Asuna was more excited than worried or frightened about this new chapter. Even the extreme new rule, that you couldn't log in again if you died, wasn't going to faze a veteran of *SAO*.

At present, the developers of *ALO*—Ymir—and many other groups were working on a solution to the situation, according to Argo. At some point, the incident would be over. Until then, she was going to help protect their home in the woods and, if possible, try to uncover the mysteries of the new world.

Sadly, Argo wasn't planning to take part in *Unital Ring* anytime soon, but her transfer to the school didn't seem unrelated to *UR*, either. Apparently, she'd had a premonition of the *UR* incident for a while now, and she made the decision to transfer to the returnee school to get closer to finding out the truth behind this event.

As always, Argo wouldn't speak about anything she didn't have evidence to back up, and they had limited time for the meeting, so that was the extent of what she reported to them. But it was clear she was going to be investigating the secrets of *Unital Ring* from the outside. When they parted ways at the school, she grinned and said that she'd leave the interior investigation to Asuna. That left no other option but to do her best.

Asuna never felt like her long commute was painful, but on this day, she finally wished that her home was closer to school. At some point, the discordant feeling in her chest had melted away.

4

"I'm home..."

As soon as I came through the entryway's glass door, I heard a voice call out, "Welcome back, Big Brother! You're late, by the way!"

Suguha was waiting in her jumpsuit on the step up to the hallway, hands clasped in front of her chest, hopping straight up and down.

"I can't help that. I have twice the commute time you do. And I raced home from the station as fast as I could."

Sure enough, even though September was coming to an end, there were huge beads of sweat on my forehead. It was nearly a mile and a half from Honkawagoe Station to the Kirigaya household, and biking that distance in six minutes had to be a new personal best. I couldn't brag about it, though, because Suguha could get home in under five, apparently. Still, my wise young sister did not insult her brother's pitiful leg strength. Instead, she offered me a face towel.

"Here you go!"

"Oh, thanks," I said, taking it and wiping my forehead.

Next there was a bottle of mineral water. "And this is for you, too!" she said, taking off the cap before handing it over.

I thanked her and downed half the bottle at once.

"Ahhh, I feel alive again..."

"Now time for another sprint!" she urged me. I rushed upstairs to my room and had just barely changed into a T-shirt and shorts when Suguha burst inside without knocking. "Are you ready?! Let's go, then!!"

In her hand was a well-used AmuSphere.

"Go? Where are you going to dive from?"

"From here, obviously! If we don't time it right, we might end up alone and in a dangerous situation."

"Don't be dramatic...It's not like the Underworld, with its time-acceleration feature. If we're off, it's only by a minute or two. Plus, Liz and Silica should already be in there."

"C'mon, just hurry!"

Suguha stuck the AmuSphere on my head, then jumped onto the bed so vigorously that the wooden slats beneath the mattress creaked. I had no choice but to lie down next to her. Suguha lifted three fingers.

"We'll go on the count of three! Three, two, one...Link Start!"

I chanted the command with her, wondering if Suguha's hand was going to drop when the device took over and flop onto my side.

Of course, I wasn't going to see it happen, even if it did.

When my eyes opened, I was staring at a ceiling of brand-new wooden boards.

Until around four in the morning, there had been a huge, gaping hole through to the sky, but there wasn't a single trace of it anymore. The log cabin, our beloved forest home that got ripped out of New Aincrad from the very foundation and suffered such terrible damage in the crash to earth, had been successfully repaired with the extra help of Lisbeth and Silica.

That's great. I'm so glad, I thought, rolling back over, when something smacked my side.

"Come on, Kirito, get up! We've got a whooooole lot of stuff to do!"

"Yeah, yeah..."

I sat up, which loudly clanked the iron armor Lisbeth had crafted for me, and looked to the side. There was Suguha's avatar, Leafa, dressed in a simple, one-piece cloth dress.

I looked around the room. The living room was much more spacious now that all the furniture was gone, and there were no other players present. Asuna was probably on her way home still. While the other four of us were at school, Alice and Yui were supposed to be protecting the cabin. Where were they now?

No sooner had the question entered my mind than a high-pitched metallic *clang!* sounded outside the window. It was not the sound of a hammer striking an anvil...It was a sword fight.

"What's that?!"

I bolted to my feet, opened the door, and hurried outside.

There in our front yard, surrounded by a variety of crafting stations, were two figures swinging swords at each other. The time in *Unital Ring* was synced up with the real world, so the setting sun was red in the distance ahead of me, making it hard to see who it was. One of the silhouettes was about my height, but the other was much smaller, like a child.

"Yaaaa!"

The childlike figure issued a fierce bellow and swung down a sword with two hands. The speed was impressive, but the adult figure comfortably blocked the swing with a one-handed parry. There was another loud clang. Thick blond braids shone, dazzling, in the light of the setting sun.

At last, I realized that the adult was Alice. And the black-haired girl fearlessly attacking the most powerful Integrity Knight ever was none other than my daughter with Asuna, the world's greatest top-down AI, Yui.

"H-hey, what's going on...?"

Without thinking, I tried to insert myself in the fight, and Leafa grabbed my shoulder.

"Wait. Isn't she training?"

"T-training...?"

I glanced at my sister, then back to the center of the yard.

It was true that Alice was receiving and blocking Yui's attacks, but she wasn't striking back at all. In fact, with each blow, she seemed to be giving small bits of advice.

"See? It's fine," Suguha said.

"Y-yeah...," I agreed, although I couldn't remember ever seeing Yui holding a weapon...except for the one time she'd used a GM weapon against the ultrapowerful boss monster the Fatal Scythe in the underground labyrinth of the first floor of Aincrad. But now Yui was treated like a player and had an HP bar like the rest of us. Alice didn't even need to fight back; she could potentially hurt herself with her own sword. I was in a state of near panic as I watched the scene unfold.

Yui finished listening intently to Alice's advice, then took her distance again. She held up her short sword, which had some rather exotic decoration on it, in a basic mid-level stance...

"Yaaaa!"

Despite her young age, she cried out fiercely as she charged. I couldn't help but make a note of surprise.

When beginners to VRMMOs attacked with a sword, they tended to perform a two-stage action: pull back, then swing down. There were situations where that was exactly the right move to do, but in almost any case, condensing the start and finish of the swing into one motion provided better speed and power. Yui's slash was firmly in line with this theory, and in fact, Alice had to pull back her left foot half a step to defend it.

Another clear, high clash of metal on metal filled the yard. The two came to a stop, then separated again.

"That was a very good one, Yui," Alice assessed. I clapped in admiration, drawing their attention. Alice seemed a little bashful, while Yui just flashed a huge smile.

"Papa! Welcome back!" she cried and started trotting toward me, still brandishing the short sword.

I had to hold out my hand. "Whoa, whoa, put that thing away first."

"Oh! Of course!"

She screeched to a halt, then slid the weapon into the sheath on her left side. Now she was free to leap into my arms, where I lifted her high overhead before nestling her in my left elbow.

"Thanks, Yui," I said. "So...why are you practicing with a sword...?"

"To fight, of course! My proficiency with One-Handed Sword skills just reached 7!"

"Oh yeah? You've been working hard," I encouraged, stroking her head. Yui giggled delightedly.

My One-Handed Sword skill, which I brought over from *ALO*, was at the maximum value of 1,000, but all the other new skills I'd gained were only at 2 or 3. For a single day's work, getting her skill up to 7 was a lot of dedication.

"If you're up that high, maybe you can use a sword skill by now," I suggested.

"Ummm..."

Yui opened her ring menu and moved to the skill window to check.

"Oh! It says I can use Vertical and Horizontal and Slant!"

"There you go. Those three are the foundation of all sword skills. Once your proficiency gets higher, I can teach you about the cooler ones, like Vorpal Strike and Howling Octave."

"Yay!" Yui exclaimed.

"About that, Kirito," said another voice, drawing my attention away. It was Alice, coming closer in her white dress, looking somewhat upset.

"Hey, Alice. Thanks for watching the house and tutoring Yui. So...what did you want to say?"

"Take a look at your skill window."

"Huh? Uh...okay..."

I drew a circle in the air with my finger. The ring menu appeared with a jingling sound, and I picked the SKILLS icon. The window that appeared had a list of acquired skills, arranged by proficiency, so of course at the top was the One-Handed Sword category...

"...Huh?"

I stared at the proficiency number in shock. When I checked this screen yesterday, it was definitely at the maximum of 1,000, but now that number was missing a zero.

"A...a hundred?! Why...?"

"Apparently, last night, when the grace period ended, the proficiency of whatever skills we brought over was lowered as well. Along with that, it made all the advanced sword skills impossible to use."

"No way..." I groaned. Leafa checked her own window and exclaimed "Oh no! Me too!" We hung our heads together, brother and sister, but I forced myself to rally.

"W-wait just a second...We fought those PKers last night *after* the grace period finished, right? I'm pretty sure I used Vorpal Strike at the time. That's supposed to be a pretty advanced skill."

"Look at your list of sword skills," Alice stated.

At her suggestion, I tapped on ONE-HANDED SWORD SKILLS. The sub-window it loaded showed the sword skills I could currently use. At the top were the basic single-attack skills: Vertical, Horizontal, and Slant; below them were the two-part Vertical Arc and Horizontal Arc. Then there was the low charging skill Rage Spike; the high-jumping skill Sonic Leap; the three-part Sharp Nail...and that was the last of them that was lit up. Below that, Vertical Square was grayed out, and tapping it opened a pop-up that said *Required proficiency: 150.* The numbers being different from *SAO* and *ALO* was understandable, but this didn't explain why I was able to use the advanced skill Vorpal Strike earlier.

I scrolled through the list and found Vorpal Strike a considerable way down, grayed out. The required proficiency was...700. That was miles above my current number of 100.

"What does that mean...? Was I simply recreating the movement on my own...?" I muttered.

But from my arm, Yui replied, "When you used Savage Fulcrum and Vorpal Strike in the battle yesterday, they had proper visual effects. That means you didn't simply mimic the motions."

"That's what I figured," I agreed, then handed Yui over to Leafa and took a position in the center of the yard. I drew my fine iron longsword, which was simply made but had a satisfying weight, and dropped my center of gravity. I extended my left hand forward and pulled the sword back in my right until it was over my shoulder—but the pre-effect of the sword skill did not arrive.

"Uryaa!" I shouted stubbornly, whipping the sword forward, but it merely ended in a thrust. There was no bloodred Vorpal Strike flash, nor even a hint of that giant jet-engine roar. I tried it again…and again. The result was the same.

"Kirito, this is really pathetic," Alice groaned.

"Y-yeah, I know that!" I snapped back childishly. I gave it a fourth try for good measure.

Shwoaaaaa-shakiiiing!!

"Wh-whaaaa—?!"

Blazing crimson, the sword shot forward, dragging me behind it. I flew ten feet through the air, then landed right on my chest.

"Gwurf!"

In the upper left corner, my HP bar decreased the tiniest bit. I groaned, limbs splayed out like a frog, until Alice rushed over and offered her hand.

"A-are you all right?!"

"Yeah…somehow…"

Once she'd helped me to my feet, I stared at the sword in my hand. Then I looked to her and murmured, "That was it just now, right? Vorstrike…"

"I must say, I do not much approve of your real-worlder customs of abbreviating everything," she said crossly. I gave her a hasty "My b," which made her glare turn even icier.

"It did activate…I'll admit that," she said. "I wonder what it means…"

"You try it, too, Alice!" said Yui from Leafa's arms. Alice glanced over at her, murmured her assent, then drew the sword from her waist. It had the same design as my sword, so it had to have been Liz's work again.

I backed away until I was standing next to Leafa. Then Alice took a stance with the blade held upright in front of her face.

Back in the Underworld, where she was born, the sword skills imported into the system from *SAO* existed as "special techniques." That made her capable of using a great variety of moves right away in *ALO*. But she seemed to prefer the one-hit-kill types, rather than speedy combo skills. It seemed like she was going to attempt the advanced One-Handed Sword skill Gelid Blade.

Her left foot stepped forward, and her sword jutted behind her to the right. Normally, performing this action would cause bluish-purple effects to surround the sword, but nothing happened.

Undaunted, Alice shouted, "Yaaaa!" and thrust the sword forward. It was a tremendous slash, but no Gelid Blade resulted. She pulled the sword back and traced that exact motion once again. Two, three, four times she attempted it, to no avail. I was starting to wonder if the Vorpal Strike I pulled off was more a bug in the system.

But then, around the seventh or eighth thrust, a light like blue fire burst through Alice's sword. She stepped forward and slashed. A tremendous cracking like the breaking of a glacier filled the air, and a bluish-purple path flickered in the air. That was the effect of Gelid Blade.

"Huh? It worked!" exclaimed Leafa. I nodded eagerly. I couldn't tell if it was a bug or a feature yet, but this suggested that if you stubbornly tried often enough, you could execute advanced sword skills even if you didn't have the required proficiency. The chances of success seemed no higher than 10 or 20 percent, however. That was too risky to try in a real battle, and I felt bad not understanding why it was happening.

First I looked to Yui over in Leafa's arms—but she was just another player now, with no special system access. I'd have to actually use my own smarts to figure this out for once.

Then Yui suggested, "Papa, perhaps the cause of this anomaly is not the player or item but the place."

I pointed at my feet and asked, "P-place? You mean this clearing has some special properties or something?"

"No, not the clearing..."

Her eyes moved, and I followed them to the site of the repaired log cabin, lit by the bronzed rays of the setting sun. I picked up on what she was suggesting and trotted over to the building so I could tap the wall. The first line of the properties window that appeared was *Cypress Log Cabin*, followed by the names of me and Asuna, its owners, then a colored bar indicating durability. It should have been fully restored this morning, but the numbers under the bar right now read *12,433/12,500*, suggesting that buildings in the world of *Unital Ring* naturally degraded over time. That was unfortunate, but the pace seemed to be around 120 points per day, so it should last for a hundred days even if we did nothing to help it.

At the bottom of the window were four buttons, reading INFO, TRANSACTION, REPAIR, and BREAK DOWN. I was certain I would never press either the TRANSACTION or BREAK DOWN buttons, so I tried INFO. Alice, Leafa, and Yui leaned over my shoulders to watch.

The sub-window that sprang to life displayed a brief description of the house, including numerical values like floor and storage space and defensive strength against various properties. At the bottom was a field labeled SPECIAL EFFECTS.

That had to be it, I decided. There was just one item listed there. It read as follows: *Level-1 / Protection of the Forest: Within a radius of 100 feet of the center of the building, the owner and any friends or party members have a small chance of executing attack skills whose requirements are not yet met.*

"Ahhh...that explains it," I murmured and rubbed Yui's little head. "Your guess was exactly correct. Did this Protection of the Forest thing exist in *ALO*, too...?"

"No, this system did not exist in *ALO*," she said, shaking her head.

Leafa interjected, "Hey, see how it says 'level-1'? Does that mean there are special effects that are level-2 and level-3?"

"I would…assume so. But I can't imagine how you would unlock those effects," I said.

Alice glanced over and suggested, "Couldn't we build them into being? The way we are building up ourselves."

"Like…raising the house's stats? How?"

"By increasing the rooms or fortifying the structure. When I built the cabin in the woods near Rulid, I started with just a simple shack with walls and a roof and built it larger from there."

"O-oh yeah? Interesting…"

My response was more than a little awkward, but I couldn't help that. Alice spent months in that cabin taking care of me while I was in a catatonic state, from what I was told. I didn't remember that time, except for the vaguest memories of being fed with a spoon and being tucked into bed. The topic filled me with a mixture of gratitude and embarrassment.

"A-anyway, this is clearly the cause of the advanced sword skills working. I must have been really lucky that I used that Vorpal Strike and got it to work the very first time last night."

"And that gives us one more thing to do," said Leafa to my confusion. She saw the look on my face and explained, "Leveling-up the house! I'm so curious what special effects are at level-2 and level-3!"

"Oh…right. Sure, that makes sense," I agreed, although I felt some resistance to the idea of expanding the log cabin. I knew better than anyone else how much love and work Asuna had put into this house, ever since the *SAO* days.

But Yui could see right through my hesitation. She stated, "It's fine, Papa! Mama doesn't get hung up on appearances. So as long as the true nature of the house remains, I don't think she'll be bothered at all!"

"What's its…true nature?"

"That's obvious! Being a place where you and Mama, and me, and Leafa, Liz, Silica, and Sinon can relax and be at peace!"

"…Uh-huh. That's true," I agreed, nodding slowly. I rubbed Yui's head one more time. "But…I think any expansion is going to be a long way ahead of us. First we need to focus more on defending the whole lot..."

I took a wide view of the clearing, a space fifty feet across, smack in the middle of deep, dense forest. The eastern half of the clearing was taken up by the log cabin, and the western half was filled with large crafting stations like a smelting furnace, a casting table, and a bisque firing kiln. These stations were easy to create as long as you had the materials, but getting those materials was a different matter. So I wanted to protect the entire clearing, if possible. While we were at school today, Yui, Alice, and Asuna's pet, Aga, the long-billed giant agamid, watched over the cabin. But if another disaster like the thornspike cave bear or the pack of hostile players attacked, the three of them would not have been successful.

The proud lady knight knew that as well and looked around the clearing with me before opining, "First we'll want a wall around the outer edge of the clearing. Preferably stone, not wood."

"True...but who knows how much stone that'll take, if we're talking about the whole rim. If only we had the glorious Administrator here. She could build us a wall of thick steel with the snap of her fingers, I bet..."

Mentioning the name of the living god who created the Everlasting Walls, which split the human realm—all thousand miles or so—into four equal parts using nothing but sacred arts earned me a chilly glare from Alice.

"Go ahead. Ask the pontifex to perform a menial task like that. She'll turn you into a cricket."

"You sure? I feel like she'd help us out if we offered her a delicious piece of cake or three."

Isn't that right, Eugeo? I thought.

With a pang, I shook my head to dispel the image of my late friend. Alice brought us a message from Dr. Koujiro of Rath yesterday, a coded message saying *The twenty-ninth, at fifteen o'clock. The expensive cake shop.* But the true sender of that message was almost certainly not Dr. Koujiro. To learn the truth of what she meant, I would have to go to a fancy café in Ginza at three in the afternoon tomorrow. It occurred to me now that tomorrow was a school day. To get from school in West Tokyo to Ginza Station, I'd have to take the Seibu Shinjuku Line to Takadanobaba, switch to the Tozai Line subway, then transfer to the Ginza Line at Nihonbashi. That was an eighty-minute trip, so I couldn't possibly make it unless I ditched my afternoon classes.

Why would you pick that specific time? I wanted to yell. But that was for tomorrow. For now, not having the almighty superpowers of the godlike pontifex, I would have to collect the materials for our wall the slow and boring way.

Fortunately, we already knew that you didn't have to stack rocks one at a time to build a wall. Within the crafting menu for the Beginner Carpentry skill was a listing for *Crude Stone Wall.* The adjective *crude* wasn't exactly appealing, but we'd have to deal with it until the skill proficiency got higher.

"So...shall we go to the riverbed to look for rocks?" I suggested, closing the cabin's properties window. Alice, Leafa, and Yui agreed to join me.

"While we're gone, we'll leave Aga to guard...Wait. Where did he go?"

I glanced around the clearing, but there was no sight of Aga, the long-billed giant agamid. At first, I was afraid that his taming period had worn off, and he'd gone wild again. Asuna would be furious! But just at that moment, there was a characteristic "*Quack!*" from behind me. I spun around and saw Aga on the southern path to the river, hopping along with Silica and Lisbeth in tow.

When the pair noticed me and Leafa, they trotted over to us.

"Kirito, what took you so long?! Did you stop somewhere to eat on the way home?!" Liz snapped, fixing me with a glare.

Silica, meanwhile, smiled awkwardly. "Kirito has a lengthy commute. That's just how long it takes him to get home."

Aga opened its bill and quacked. On its head was Pina, who squeaked, though it was hard to tell which one of the two girls they were agreeing with. In any sense, Aga was still clearly tamed and friendly.

"Where were you two just now?" I asked.

Liz rubbed Aga's neck and replied, "This little guy loses HP if he doesn't get a couple dunks in the water throughout the day. So we went to the river and collected some rocks while we were there."

"Oh, that's great. For being a lizard, this thing's pretty needy, huh…?"

"Papa, there are plenty of half-aquatic lizards in the real world, too. Like the Mertens' water monitor or the Sulawesi crocodile skink," Yui noted promptly. I murmured with surprise, but then I recalled that the first time we encountered Aga, it was coming out of the river. And that duck-like bill was evidence that it was aquatic in nature.

"Well, we need to dig a well pretty soon, then. There's so much to do!"

I shook my head and checked the clock in the lower right. It was 5:50 PM. I couldn't stay in this dive all the way to dawn this time, so if I logged off at midnight or at two in the morning that would give me a bit over eight hours. I was almost feeling a little wistful for the days of *SAO*, when I could spend my entire day tackling the challenges of the game.

A deep breath helped me dispel that thought. I was going to head to the river for those stones when Leafa stepped in front of me, still carrying Yui.

"Big Brother, shouldn't we prioritize meeting up with Sinon instead? In the long run, more hands will make the work go faster, and more fighting power will be reassuring."

"Hmm. You're not wrong…," I said reluctantly.

At the after-school meeting, Sinon delivered several pieces of stunning news. Numerous players from her home game of *Gun Gale Online* were converted into *Unital Ring* as well. That wasn't particularly surprising, but the fact that they were able to bring in guns was.

Of course, we *ALO* players brought our swords and spears in, so it stood to reason that *GGO* players could have their weapons. That was only fair—but theirs were *guns*. And in *GGO*, there weren't just gunpowder-based guns but also optical guns that shot lasers. How did the mysterious mastermind of this incident expect to manage the logical integrity of combining such wildly different worlds?

But that wasn't something we needed to worry about for now. Sinon's Hecate II was an ultrapowerful gun that was the equivalent of a top-tier thirty-word attack spell in *ALO*. Apparently, she'd lost almost all her ammo, but if you could have a gun here, there had to be a way to replenish them, and if we could meet up with her, she'd be a huge benefit to our mutual defense.

But the biggest problem was…

"We don't even know which direction to find this village of birdpeople where Sinon is…," I lamented, shoulders dropping.

"She said she didn't even notice the sound or shock wave of New Aincrad falling," said Silica worriedly. "That would suggest the *GGO* players started somewhere very distant from our initial location."

"Hmm…"

Meanwhile, Lisbeth opened her ring menu and tapped the MAP icon in the lower left. The map it displayed was colored in with a much wider range than mine or Leafa's.

"Let's see," she said. "This is the ruins where the *ALO* players started, right? And New Aincrad's crash landing was here. The village of the Bashin is north of that, and way to the northeast is this cabin…Silica and I walked here from the village, but we didn't see any giant dinosaurs or centipede monsters like Sinon described."

Silica nodded, then noticed something and ran her finger over the map. "But when we were walking from the Bashin village, it started as wasteland and gradually turned into grassland, and then forest once we crossed the river. Sinon said her area was a desert with no water anywhere, so it seems like a higher probability that she's in the opposite direction of the forest."

"Uh-huh…," murmured Leafa, Alice, and I. Silica had a good point, but even if she was right about the direction, we couldn't go searching blindly without knowing a rough distance. There were stamina points and thirst points to manage here, in addition to HP, and that meant we needed plenty of food and water to complete the trip.

No sooner had the thought entered my mind than I felt slightly conscious of my empty stomach and dry throat. Thankfully, the game preserved the points' status while we were offline, so my bars were down only about 20 percent for SP and 30 percent for TP, but they would go quickly once we started working. We had a nearby river for water and plenty of bear meat left for food, but we needed a more stable source of that soon.

"We'll need to chop down some trees and till a field…assuming we can actually do that in this game," I muttered.

"I'll add it to the list of things to do," Yui noted studiously.

"Th-thanks…Uh, so how's that list looking now?"

"I haven't put them in any priority, but it's currently looking like: build a defensive wall, expand the log cabin, make weapons and armor for everyone, raise levels, tame stronger monsters, dig a well, cultivate a field, meet up with Sinon, and reach the land revealed by the heavenly light!"

"………"

The group shared a silent look. The last one on that list would indeed have to be saved for last, but everything else was a high priority right now.

"…Let's start with the defensive wall," I said, recovering my initiative.

Lisbeth nodded. "That's what we figured and why we brought lots of stones back with us. I'll try to make a wall and see what happens."

"Thanks, that'd be great."

Liz shot me a thumbs-up, then closed her map and opened the skill window instead. From the list of craftable items under the Beginner Carpentry skill, she chose *Stacked Rock Wall*, bringing up a translucent light-purple ghost object. Awkwardly, she slid the ghost along until it stopped at the boundary between the clearing and forest.

"Can I make it here?" she asked.

"Hang on," I said, then walked up next to the see-through stone wall, checking the placement and angle carefully. "Can you push it, like, six inches back…and rotate a teensy bit to the right?"

"L-like this?" Liz angled her fingers slightly, and the ghost crawled forward. When it was in just the right spot, I shouted "There!"

Liz squeezed her hand shut, and a number of gray rocks tumbled out of thin air and landed perfectly in the place of the ghost wall. The actual wall that resulted was about five feet tall and long and one foot thick. The rocks of various sizes were packed without any gaps, so it didn't feel as slapdash as I was afraid it would. Just to test, I gave it a push, but it didn't jar any rocks loose.

"This actually looks like it can help protect against monsters somewhat," I stated, patting the wall.

Alice looked a bit conflicted. "True…but I doubt it will stop the charge of a thornspike cave bear, and any player will be able to climb over."

"We'll just have to pray we don't have any teddy bears wandering our way for a while. But as for the players…" I said, turning to Lisbeth. "How many of your stones did you use for this block of wall, Liz?"

"Hmm. I used thirty favillite rocks—that's the most common one at the river—and five pieces of rough gray clay."

"And how much do you have left of both of those?"

"A hundred twenty-something rocks and twenty clay," she replied.

Silica raised her hand. "I've got a hundred stones and fifteen clay, too!"

"Thanks, Silica. So that means we can make another seven blocks of wall with what you two have on hand. Liz, test to see if you can put another section of wall on top of this one."

"Okeydoke," Lisbeth replied and opened the window again. When she slid the second ghost wall over toward the first, it snapped into place, initially latching onto its right edge. When she tried to push it to the left, the ghost popped over and stacked itself atop the first.

"Oh, I think it works."

"Awesome. Do that."

Da-doom! With another heavy rumble, the new wall fell on top of the first one. Now it was ten feet tall. It wasn't perfectly impervious, but it would cause all but the most nimble players to think twice before climbing.

Of course, in its current state, it was less of a wall than a very flat pillar. The clearing was fifty feet in diameter, which made its circumference close to 160 feet. To circle the entire space, we'd want thirty-two blocks, then, which would be sixty-four when double-stacked. I didn't even want to calculate how much favillite we'd need for that…

That was when the door of the log cabin burst open, and Asuna leaped through, wearing a white dress.

"Sorry, everyone! I didn't mean to be late!"

"No, Asuna, you've got good timing! What's sixty-four times thirty?!" I asked promptly.

Asuna looked confused at first but immediately answered, "One thousand nine hundred and twenty." Then she narrowed her eyes with suspicion and asked, "Why…?"

"That's how many rocks we'll need to build that wall around the entire clearing."

I pointed out the gray wall standing near the smelting furnace.

"Ohhh," she exclaimed, catching on.

"Big Brother, are you really not able to do that calculation in your head?" murmured Leafa with concern.

We headed for the riverbed as a group and collected as much favillite and clay by the light of the setting sun as we could. After returning to the cabin, Liz and I spent an hour using our Beginner

Carpentry skill to make sections of wall, one after another. By the time we had finished placing a wall ten feet high around the entire clearing, the sun had set all the way.

As a matter of fact, the wooden gates we built on the northern and southern ends meant that the number of stones we used was a bit below Asuna's calculated sum—but it was still a mammoth task. But the satisfaction of finishing the wall was tremendous, and we celebrated with plenty of high fives, even from Alice.

"It really feels so much more secure with a wall!" commented Silica once we'd settled down a little.

"That's right," I agreed. "I wonder if the ancient Greeks felt like this when they completed a wall around their cities."

"It's not *quite* as large as Athens or Corinth," snarked Asuna, but I just flashed a grin back at her.

"You don't know that. We'll keep building and building until, eventually, it's a city the size of Athens—or even Centoria."

Now it was Alice's turn to join the fun. "Oh? A bold claim. I am looking forward to seeing it."

"I...I've got it under control," I boasted, thumping my chest, before quickly changing the topic. "Anyway, that's one item off our list of tasks. Next up is..."

"Ooh! Ooh, ooh, ooh!" hollered Leafa, waving her arm. "I want a sword and armor, too!"

"...Yeah, good point..."

With myself decked out in full iron armor, it wouldn't be fair to deny her that request. Liz and Silica had leather armor and metal weapons they'd received from the Bashin, but poor Leafa and Asuna were still wearing ubiquigrass dresses and wielding a stone ax and a stone knife, respectively.

Fortunately, we had Liz, who'd inherited her Blacksmithing skill from *ALO*, so the technical aspect was taken care of. The problem was all the ore we'd need to smelt. We'd found a lot of ore in the thornspike cave bear's lair last night and recovered some iron equipment from the PKers, but virtually all of it had gone to repairing the cabin. We'd have to return to the bear's cave to get more ore, but the owner had surely respawned by now, and it'd taken a desperate gambit of dropping tons of logs onto it from the roof of the cabin to kill the first one. That wouldn't work twice, I knew.

"Yui, did the Bashin mention where they got their ore?" I asked.

The AI was the only one of us able to understand the mysterious NPC language, but she just shook her head. "I'm sorry, Papa. I wasn't able to learn that information..."

"You don't have to apologize. It's my fault for forgetting to ask where to find ore when they were showing us the source of silica and flax. We'll figure it out."

"That's right, Yui. Kirito will figure it out," Asuna said, picking up Yui and giving her a nurturing smile.

Yui smiled back, but she still looked worried. "What exactly are you going to do, Papa?"

"Beat the thornspike cave bear the orthodox way, of course... Though, hold on." I turned to look at Silica, who was sitting to my right with Pina on her head. "The best outcome would be to tame it, rather than kill it. That would probably stop it from repopulating each time."

"What?! Tame a bear?!" she exclaimed, pulling back.

I grinned. "Asuna doesn't even have the Beast-Taming skill, and she turned that duck-dino into a pet. You inherited the skill from back in *ALO*, so a bear should be easy-peasy for you..."

"Unfortunately, Kirito, the skill I inherited was Daggers."

"What? Really? Your proficiency was higher in the Daggers skill?" I exclaimed, surprised.

Silica pouted, pursing her lips. "Kirito, raising the Beast-Taming skill to a proficiency of 1,000 is incredibly hard. From what I know, the only person in *ALO* to max it out is Alicia, the master of the cait siths."

"Oh, I'm sorry for my ignorance...So that means Asuna actually has a higher Beast-Taming skill at this point..."

I looked at her, but she just blinked and shook her head. "N-no, don't look at me! I can't tame that horrible bear," she protested.

Even so, I was busy thinking of how to trick—er, convince—her to achieve that feat when Silica announced, "I-if you're just going to force Asuna to attempt something dangerous, *I'll* do it!"

Either she was feeling bold, thanks to the armor from the Bashin, or I'd wounded her beast-tamer's pride. Asuna tried to say something, but Silica held out her hands to push her back down. "No, Asuna, it's fine. I didn't see this bear, but in terms of beast-taming, it's got to be a lower difficulty than bug-types or demon-types. I'll work up my Beast-Taming skill again and bend that beast to my will!"

It's probably not the kind of bear you're imagining, I thought. Asuna and Leafa and Alice were probably thinking the same thing. Before anyone could say anything contrary, I stepped forward and grasped Silica by the shoulders.

"Yes! That's the Silica I know—the idol of all beast-tamers in *SAO*! It's a huge relief to hear you guarantee that!"

"Heh-heh-heh…I'll do my best," she replied, laughing self-consciously. Over Silica's shoulder, I could see Asuna sighing, but I wasn't going to slow down now.

"Asuna, can you teach Silica how to get the Beast-Taming skill? There was that fox monster in the woods when we were on the way back from the river, so that's probably a good practice target. Me, Liz, Alice, and Leafa will dig up a well before we run out of TP again."

"That sounds good…but are you sure we can just dig wherever we want in this game?" Lisbeth asked.

That gave me pause. In most VRMMOs, including *ALO*, it was impossible to change the landscape of the wilderness. It would invalidate the map design, after all, and players would be digging giant holes all over the place just to mess with one another.

Unital Ring wasn't a normal game in many respects, but I had a hard time imagining you could alter the terrain here…and I'd been thinking about this yesterday, too. But on the other hand, in the Beginner Carpentry skill's production menu was…

"Look…a well," I said, pointing at the opened menu for the

others to see. Just as I remembered from the list, there was an entry that said *Small Stacked Rock Well.*

"Doesn't that mean it's like the smelting furnace, where if you place it, you can have a well wherever you want?" asked Leafa, but I wasn't buying it.

"You really think it's that simple? If you can create a well anytime you want, as long as you have the materials, that totally invalidates the point of the TP bar."

"Don't complain to me—I didn't invent it. Anyway, why don't you just test it out?"

That was a good point. I checked the type and number of materials needed for the well: three hundred stones, twenty sawed logs, ten clay, fifty iron nails, one iron chain.

"Ugh, we don't have anywhere near what we need. It's easy enough to get the stones and the logs, but the iron..."

"It's not going to be easy," said Alice, shrugging. She glanced at the furnace. "No matter what, we're going to need iron. It's going to take time for Silica's beast-taming project to come through. Will we have to fight another thornspike cave bear?"

"Hmm...In a normal game, I'd just go for broke and try to fight it anyway, but now..."

I hemmed and hawed, and Alice and the others frowned.

In *Unital Ring*, dying meant you could never log in again. But it wouldn't spit you back out in *ALO*, either. The VRMMO worlds stuck in the incident were overwritten on the server side and effectively shut down to the public. Devs attempted to roll back a few of the games, but even if the Seed program were reinstalled, they wouldn't function, according to Argo. Under these circumstances, even I, the triple-crown winner of insane, reckless gambles, was not up to fighting the ultrapowerful thornspike cave bear.

"Iron...ironnnn..."

I folded my arms and stared up at the night sky. In *SAO* and *ALO*, iron weapons and tools were in ready supply in even the earliest towns, so it never felt that valuable. Monsters would drop tons of iron items, so I regularly threw away whatever I couldn't carry. Now I wished I could go back in time to pick up all that excess supply.

If I searched hard enough in the area nearby, I could probably find some iron ore in a location aside from the bear cave. But considering the general rules of game difficulty, it seemed that the rarity of iron ore was set to "strong enough to defeat a thornspike cave bear with relative ease." I shouldn't expect a steady supply of ore on the open sides of hills. The true Iron Age was not going to arrive unless we could deal with that bear somehow.

"...Let's look for Sinon," I murmured. Alice, Leafa, and Liz glanced at me; in the distance, Asuna, Silica, and Yui stopped talking about beast-taming to look my way, too.

In the tense silence that followed, Asuna's voice was crystal clear. "I want to meet up with Shino-non, too...but we don't know where she is or even what direction to search. How will we search for her?"

"The Bashin people they came across might know something about the birdpeople Sinon's with. We want info on ore anyway, so let's go to the Bashin village and ask them," I said, looking at the rest of the group in order. "Asuna, Silica, Alice, you stay here and protect the cabin. I'll go with Leafa, Liz, and Yui to the village...How does that sound?"

"I understand that Asuna and Silica have the Beast-Taming skill to discuss, but why are you leaving me here?" demanded Alice, sounding disgruntled.

"Because if you're here watching the house, I feel confident it's safe," I said honestly.

"...In that case...I cannot argue. Very well...but I will insist on taking part in the next expedition," she announced, turning on her heel and lining up with Asuna and Silica.

Asuna put her hand on Alice's back, and in a crisp, clear voice that reminded me of when she was the vice commander of the Knights of the Blood, she said, "We will keep our home safe, so make sure you return home safe, too. That's a promise."

"...It is," I agreed. Liz added, "We'll bring Sinon back with us!" and Yui rushed over to hug Asuna. While that was happening, I opened my inventory to test something I'd been thinking about.

I brought out the longsword Blárkveld, which I'd transferred over from our home storage. My special sword from *ALO* was still too costly to equip; even at level-13, I couldn't use it yet. With my window open, I walked toward Lisbeth.

"Liz...I hate to ask this after you made it for me, but could you melt down this sword?"

"What?" the forger of Blárkveld exclaimed, stunned. "W-well, you're the owner, so you can do what you want with it...but there's no guarantee I can make you a sword of the same rank now that we're stuck in *this* world."

"I know that. But I think I'll need to get to level-40 or level-50 to use this thing. If it's just going to waste away in storage, I'd rather melt it down and put it to good use for the group."

"...Hmm. All right." She grinned, then reached for the black sword resting atop the window.

"Oh, hold on! Remember, if you touch it, it'll fall to the ground, and then you can't move it."

"Ah, right."

"Hang on—I'll put it directly into the furnace."

With my inventory still open, I walked over to the western side of the clearing, opened the operating window of the smelting furnace, and dropped Blárkveld inside. The sword floating in the air vanished, scattering motes of light. Then I set firewood in the furnace's combustion chamber and let Lisbeth take over from there.

The blacksmith briefly placed her hands together to pray for the sword she forged herself, then used a flintstone to light the logs. Soon there were flickering red flames inside, and a roaring sound escaped the furnace as they burned furiously.

Last night, the iron ore began to melt in just a few dozen seconds after I set the logs in the furnace, but Blárkveld resisted the flames for nearly two minutes. But at last, molten metal shining white escaped the spigot and filled the ingot mold. When it was full, the metal flashed and vanished so that the mold could fill again.

It was only a one-handed sword in there, so I figured that getting ten ingots out of it would be a success, but in *Unital Ring*, it seemed that high-ranked gear also increased the number of materials you could salvage from it. The molten iron flowed and flowed and only stopped after I had given up keeping track of the count.

"...It's over," Lisbeth murmured, opening the furnace's window. "Let's see. We got...sixty-two premium steel ingots, eighteen fine silver ingots, nine fine meteoric iron ingots, six mythril ingots, and two black dragon steel ingots."

"Wowww...Some of those sound really rare," Leafa whispered with great reverence. If Blárkveld gave us this much stuff, what would happen if I melted down the Holy Sword, Excalibur, the other weapon I brought over from *ALO*? Not that melting down the legendary weapon that I went through such trouble to gain was anything but a last resort, of course.

Instead, I asked Liz, "Can you make equipment for Alice, Asuna, and Leafa with this stuff?"

"Hmm...Remember, my Blacksmithing skill went down to 100, too. I might not be able to use the fancier metal," she muttered with consternation, moving the ingots to her own inventory, then sitting at the little chair in front of the anvil. She dropped a premium steel ingot on the anvil's window and opened the crafting menu.

"Oh, looks like I can just barely do steel weapons. So I'll make Alice's sword first. Will a bastard sword do?"

"Yes, Liz. Thank you."

"You got it."

Lisbeth flashed the knight a thumbs-up and grabbed her smithing hammer, then smacked the silvery-brown ingot that appeared atop the anvil.

As the hammer clanged against the metal, loud and crisp, I prayed that the new swords about to be born turned out as sturdy and faithful as my lost Blárkveld.

5

I'm glad I dived in without eating anything first.

Sinon stared at the chunk of meat before her, sizzling and snapping.

The rare steak was three inches thick and almost a foot in size. By real-world standards, it was so big that even a sumo wrestler would have trouble finishing it. But the birdmen seated around the gigantic table were all busy with steaks of the same size, carving with their knives and chewing vigorously.

Of course, this was a virtual world, and no matter what she ate, nothing went into her real stomach, but one of the strange features of full-diving was that the satiating feeling of a full belly lasted for a while, even after logging out. Sinon had a small appetite to begin with and wasn't the biggest fan of meat, so a rare steak of this size was a major challenge for her. Especially since it wasn't beef, or even pork.

Confirming that the birdmen on either side were completely absorbed in eating, Sinon quickly tapped the hunk of meat. The properties window said it was *Sterocephalus Tail Meat Steak*. It had previously belonged to the dinosaur she killed with a shot from the Hecate II.

Last night, Sinon had been on the brink of dying of dehydration just before reaching a pool of water. Surrounded by birdmen delighted at the defeat of their *sterocephalus* foe, she allowed them to escort her to their village.

As usual, the two sides couldn't understand a word the other said, but she received a savior's welcome in the village anyway. They showed her to a pretty little house in the center of the village, where she was able to log out safely. This evening, she drank some water as soon as she got home and promptly dived back in, where they more or less forced her into this celebration.

What surprised her a little—no, a lot—was the high level of civilization the birdmen enjoyed. The houses of the village were neatly arranged and built with fired bricks, and the perfectly circular outer edge of the village was surrounded by a sturdy stone wall. The tiled streets led to a large meeting space in the center of the village that was surrounded by shops.

She shouldn't have been this surprised, she realized, because the fact that they used muskets already spoke to a culture of a certain level. So if she left the majority of her dinosaur steak, maybe they would be civilized enough not to be angry with her, she hoped…

"אאאא?"

A small birdperson who came up to her side poured red wine-like liquid into the glass in front of Sinon. Their words sounded like a question, but she still couldn't understand them.

"I'm sorry, I don't know what you're saying to me," she replied. The child's yellow beak hung open partway in apparent confusion. Sinon was going to apologize again when a voice cut her off.

"The child is asking why you do not eat," the voice said from her left. Sinon turned in that direction in utter shock.

The voice came from an elderly-looking birdman who had long gray feathers hanging from the edges of his beak.

"You…you understand my language?" she asked hoarsely.

One edge of the elderly birdman's beak twitched upward. "When I was younger, I adventured all over the continent with humans. But…does the dinosaur meat not suit your tastes, human girl?"

"Er, no…it's fine. Thank you," she said, summoning her courage and picking up the knife and fork. She carved a bit off the end of the singed log of a steak and popped it into her mouth.

Once her teeth bit through the crispy exterior, they met much more resilience than she expected. But a firmer bite cut through it easily enough, and a fatty sweetness filled her mouth. It tasted like beef ribs but was more fibrous and gamy. There was no sauce on the meat, but the spices the birdmen cooked it with had a kick. It wasn't bad.

"Um…how do I say *delicious* in your language?" she asked the elderly birdman. He made a sound like *hyufol*. She turned to the child and repeated the word the birdman had just taught her. The child looked befuddled.

"No. It is *hyufol*."

"Hyufol."

"Close. *Hyufol*."

"Hyufol!"

After a few repetitions like this, the child finally understood her, and she beamed and shouted, "Hyufol!" Her head bobbed up and down excitedly, and then she walked away.

Instantly, there was a window in front of Sinon's face that read *Ornith skill gained. Proficiency has risen to 1.*

She blinked, then listened to the conversations happening around her in the large room. Most of them still just sounded like strange chirping, but occasionally she heard snippets that she understood, like "Now the farm to the south will be…" and "I'll have more wine…"

In their meeting after school, Yui said that the NPC language in *Unital Ring* was actually the Seed protocol's Japanese language set but with several layers of filtering to make it impossible to understand. Most likely, thanks to gaining the Ornith skill, the game was decoding fragments of those filters now and then, so she could hear the Japanese. If she raised her proficiency further, the filter would eventually disappear altogether, she supposed.

But how to raise that proficiency? She took another bite of

dinosaur steak, chewed it briskly, and replayed the conversation before the skill pop-up appeared. Then she swallowed her food and spoke to the elderly birdman again.

"Um, how do you say *knife* in Ornith?"

"Hmm? You mean *fetu*?"

"Fetu."

"No, *fetu*."

"Fetu."

"Listen to me. It is *fetu*."

"I *am* saying *fetu*!" Sinon snapped, and another message appeared, reading *Ornith skill proficiency has risen to 2.* The same child as before ran over and offered Sinon a new knife. That settled it—raising her Ornith proficiency required repeating the undecoded words perfectly. Why did it have to be annoying?

Once again, she turned to the elder.

"...How do you say *thank you* in Ornith?"

Forty minutes later, Sinon returned from the feast to her room and flopped face-first onto the bed.

Thankfully, the birdpeople, known as Orniths, did not have any barbarous customs of searing and devouring ungrateful guests who didn't finish their food. Sinon stubbornly continued to pile dinosaur steak into her virtual stomach as she learned vocabulary words from the elder birdman, but her core was screaming at her to stop when she was only half done. Still, she must have devoured at least two pounds of it. She didn't even want to *think* about eating meat again for a while, real or virtual.

But attending the feast was certainly worthwhile, because she got her Ornith skill up to 10 and learned much more valuable information as well. She rolled over onto her back, opened the ring menu, and flicked open the MAP icon.

The image it summoned showed the ruined city where she'd started, the wasteland to the east of it, the rocky outcropping where she'd fought the giant *sterocephalus*, and the Ornith village well to the north of that. She felt like she'd covered quite a lot of ground, but if she used two fingers to zoom out on the map, the lit portions shrank smaller and smaller until they were the size of grains of sand. If that represented the full size of the entire world map, then the vast distance she'd spent hours walking across represented less than 1 percent of the game world.

The real problem wasn't the distance to the edge of the world, though, but how far away she was from Kirito and Asuna's location.

At the end of the feast, Sinon asked virtually everyone who was present if they knew about the name Bashin. When even her elderly Ornith tutor, who had traveled the world, said "Never heard of 'em," she felt desperate. But by some miracle, just one birdperson there said they'd heard the name before. So Sinon used all of her proficiency-10 Ornith skill to ask everything she possibly could.

That one birdperson had never met the Bashin, only heard a story from his grandfather, but the information in the story was worth its weight in gold: *The Bashin village is past the vast Giyoru Savanna to the southeast.* It was worth the trouble. Asuna's log cabin had fallen near the Bashin village, supposedly, so if she went southeast, she should be able to catch up to them—possibly. Of course, if the Bashin had villages all over the world map, she could easily find herself on a wild-goose chase, but for now, she could only trust that her new lead was the right one.

"...Okay!"

Sinon closed the map and sat up forcefully. She'd already told the Orniths that she would leave before the end of the night. The reason they'd been waging that hopeless fight against the ferocious *sterocephalus* was because the dinosaur was attacking their farm to the south and devouring the valuable psittacos there.

It wasn't clear what kind of livestock psittacos were, but when the Orniths learned that their new hero, vanquisher of the previously unbeatable *sterocephalus*, was leaving already, they were very disappointed. Sinon wanted to stick around and use the village as a base for leveling-up—after all, she could eat and stay for free—but more than that, she wanted to regroup with her friends. That fallen log cabin was a special place to her, too, and there wasn't much of a point to solving the mysteries of *Unital Ring* if it wasn't with Asuna and Kirito.

With the Bellatrix SL2 and Weasel Suit equipped again, Sinon left the building and looked around. Across the way, the lights were already out at the feast hall, and there was no one to be seen around the circular building. The time was only just after seven o'clock, but the Orniths did not seem to have a nightlife. No sooner had the thought occurred to her than Sinon muttered, "Dammit!" She was going to use her 100-el silver coin to buy some rations and drinking water, but all of the shops on the southern side of the village center had their shutters down. She'd been careless; NPC shops in *ALO* and *GGO* both ran essentially twenty-four hours a day, but normal VRMMO logic didn't apply here.

"...And that probably means there's no guarantee this village even takes silver el coins...," she murmured, feeling dejected. After eating and drinking as much as her willpower could possibly allow, her SP and TP were full, but she never wanted to be foolish enough to head into the wilderness without water again. Should she wait until the morning for the shops to open? Or look for a place where she could get free water...?

"Miss Sinon!"

She spun to her right at the sound of her name. There were two Orniths trotting toward her, a young one and a child. At first, they'd all looked the same to her, but now she could tell them apart to a small degree, due to the colors and patterns of their feathers and the shape of their eyes and beaks.

The young Ornith was the musketeer she'd saved from the *sterocephalus*. The child was the birdgirl who'd been serving the table at the feast. The young one lowered the plumage over his eyes and asked, "Sinon, are you already ℵℵℵ?"

Her Ornith skill was only at a proficiency of 10, so part of the sentence was unclear, but she could guess that he was asking if she was leaving now, and she nodded in response.

"Yes. I must go to the Bashin village."

He understood her response and seemed to frown, as far as she could tell. "I see...I don't ℵℵℵ anything about the Bashin, but if you are crossing the Giyoru Savanna to the southeast, you will need to prepare ℵℵ. Please take this with you, Miss Sinon."

He held out a shiny black musket. Sinon blinked, then shook her head vigorously. "No, I can't! This gun is very important to you, isn't it?"

"No!" shouted the birdgirl, who had light-brown feathers. She looked at the musket in the young birdman's hands and explained, "That isn't my brother's. It belonged to our late grandfather. Father says there's no ℵℵ anymore, so he should ℵℵ it to you for saving our village, Sinon."

"That's right. It's an old gun, but the quality is ℵℵ. Of course, it's nowhere near as fine as your gun, but you wouldn't want to use something so powerful on smaller beasts and insects, would you?"

He had a good point. She only had six of the Hecate's .50 BMG bullets left, and they had to be saved for emergencies. The Bellatrix also had only 60 percent of its energy remaining. The chances of her getting more ammunition for either were low.

"...In that case, I'd be glad to use it," Sinon said, and the young Ornith happily offered her the musket. There was a satisfying weight to it in her hands. He also gave her a leather bag slung over his shoulder.

"Those are the bullets and gunpowder. If you use them all up, the bullets can be ℵℵ from iron, and for the gunpowder, you can mix the secretions of bursting beetles and charcoal powder, then let it dry."

"B-bursting beetles?" Sinon repeated, suspicious. The birdgirl, who seemed to be the older Ornith's sister, formed a large circle with her hands.

"They're at the base of ℵℵℵℵ cacti! Just watch out, because if you step on them, they'll blow up and hurt you real bad!"

"Um...okay, I'll be careful."

Sadly, she couldn't make out the name of the cactus itself, but that was all right. She wasn't planning to go walking up to any cacti anytime soon.

Sinon slung the gun over her back, then hung the ammo bag on her shoulder. This time, it was the birdgirl who offered her yet another object, a large cloth bag.

"There's water and butter and hard bread in here! Me and Mom and Grandma made them! There's also a pelt cloak in there, so if a ℵℵ comes, use it!"

If she refused now, it would probably be rude. She was very curious about what "if a ℵℵ comes" was referring to, but she didn't want to grill the birdgirl, so she thanked her and took the sack.

The birdgirl grinned and added, "The hard bread's not very good, but it lasts a really long time! When ℵℵℵ, sear it over a fire and spread the butter on it, and it'll taste much ℵℵ!"

"...Okay, I'll try that. Thank you so much," she said, bowing one more time, then took the birdgirl's hands in her own. "Can you tell me your name?"

"Sure! I'm Fikki, and my brother is Ufelm!"

"Fikki...and Ufelm. I *will* return to this village someday. And I'll bring you many gifts from my travels."

"Yay!" Fikki exclaimed excitedly. Sinon fixed the image of the little birdgirl's excitement in her mind and swore to herself that she would uphold that promise.

It was seven thirty PM. Sinon left the Ornith village, opened her map window, and looked for a landmark that would help her head southeast. Fortunately, there was a large moon shining in the sky, and with the help of the Night Vision skill, she could make out the terrain on her own. Upon gazing to the southeast, she noticed a rock growth in the distance that looked just like a gate.

"...There we go!"

With her motivation as fuel, Sinon strode across the dried earth. She had no idea how many miles across this Giyoru Savanna was, but she was determined to cross it and reach the Bashin village by the end of the night. After all, beating the *sterocephalus* field boss had put her all the way up to level-16, and she had a musket on her back and a Bellatrix SL2 at her side.

She certainly didn't want to fight any more giant dinosaurs, but she felt confident she could beat any centipede or scorpion. Her HP was higher, her stats built up…

Right. Her stats. *Unital Ring* didn't have basic character stats like STR and AGI. Instead, it had a varied system of abilities, which served a different function from skills. With the levels she'd gained, she now had fifteen ability points to spend, and there was no point hoarding them if she was going to try crossing the dangers of the wilderness alone.

"…I'm really not good at this sort of thing," she murmured, switching from the map screen to the ability list. At the meeting after school, Kirito had said that it didn't seem like you could re-spec your abilities once chosen, which was the same way it worked in *GGO*. The problem was that there were way too many choices in *Unital Ring*.

Perhaps she should return to the Ornith village, log out in a safe spot, then look up information on the abilities online. But no… barely twenty-four hours had passed since the incident began, so it wasn't smart to believe anything you saw written on the Net at this point. She should think for herself about what she needed and make that choice on her own. That was a lesson the *GGO* player Zexceed had taught her before he was killed by Death Gun.

"…I guess I should use ten points now," Sinon murmured and lifted her finger to pick from the four starter abilities.

6

"...I'm just not good at this sort of thing," I murmured, staring at the ability screen.

Lisbeth finished drinking some water and groaned, "Just go by feeling. Leafa and I did ours really quick."

"That's the problem. I'm not good at going by feeling," I mumbled, focusing on the options.

In the center of the screen were four icons in a cross pattern. Clockwise from the top, they were BRAWN, TOUGHNESS, SAGACITY, and SWIFTNESS. Each of those icons had two lines extending farther in that direction toward more icons. Past BRAWN, there was BONEBREAKER and STOUT. Past TOUGHNESS, there was PERSEVERANCE and ANTIVENOM. Past SAGACITY, there was CONCENTRATION and LEARNED. Past SWIFTNESS, there was GALLOP and DEXTEROUS.

Tapping an icon brought up a description of the ability. According to this, Brawn gave a bonus to medium- and large-melee-weapon damage, equip weight, and carry weight. Toughness gave a bonus to HP, TP, SP, and status-ailment resistance. Sagacity gave a bonus to MP value and magic power. Swiftness gave a bonus to ranged-weapon damage, small-melee-weapon damage, and jumping distance.

In other words, the suggestion was that damage dealers should take the Brawn ability tree; tanks should go for the Toughness tree; mages, the Sagacity tree; and scouts, the Swiftness tree. As a user of a longsword, a midsize melee weapon, that meant I should take Brawn without overthinking it—but it wasn't going to be that simple. In a survival RPG, maximum HP, SP, and TP values were crucial. I could envision myself nearly dying of hunger or thirst in the future and wishing, *If only I'd maxed out Toughness back then*, at least once or twice, if not a full ten times.

I sighed and asked my friends, "Anyway…what did following your feelings lead you to pick?"

Lisbeth said, "I did Toughness," while Leafa added "Brawn for me," and Yui chimed in with "I picked Sagacity!"

That one took me by surprise. "Sagacity…? Are you going to be a magic user, Yui?" I asked.

"That's right! I want to be a battle mage just like Mama!"

"Uh…okay. That sounds reassuring."

Of course, the reason Asuna was feared far and wide as the Berserk Healer of *ALO* was because of her incredible defense and evasion techniques, but I didn't want to ruin any child's dreams, so I patted Yui's head instead. After all, there was no way to rule out the possibility, and it was my duty to protect her, regardless of what build she went with.

In that sense, perhaps a tank would be best, I thought, losing myself in choice once again. When we'd left the cabin, there'd still been some sunset light in the western part of the sky, but that was long gone now, replaced by dark clouds that flowed in front of the faded stars.

"Hmm, if only I knew the effects of the second row of abilities…"

I could only read the descriptions of the currently selectable abilities, so I'd have to actually make a choice to find out more.

Leafa was munching on some nuts across the way, and she asked archly, "Have you considered asking *us* what they are…?"

"Huh…? Oh, d-duh…"

They had already picked their first ability, so they would be able to read the description of the next options. I cleared my throat, feeling awkward, and turned to the other three.

"If you don't mind the trouble, would you please tell me what comes next?"

"If you insist," Liz said with a sigh, opening her ring menu. "Let's see. The abilities past Toughness are Perseverance, which gives a bonus to damage-reduction when guarding, and Antivenom, which gives a bonus to damage-reduction against poison, as you'd guess."

"Mm-hmm."

Next, Leafa checked her window. "The abilities after Brawn are Bonebreaker, which provides a bonus to damage that ignores enemy guarding, and Stout, which gives you decreased knock-back when guarding."

"Hmm…?"

Yui didn't need to check her window first. "The abilities stemming from Sagacity are Concentration, which gives a bonus to MP recovery rate, and Learned, which increases proficiency gain of all language skills."

"Hmmmm."

Language skills probably referred to the skills that let you speak with NPCs, but I wouldn't need that if Yui was around. I didn't intend to be a mage, so I removed the Sagacity tree from my set of options. But even knowing what came after Brawn and Toughness, it was hard to pick between them.

"Hmm. It sounds like Stout and Perseverance are fairly similar. Why are the abilities for knockback-reduction and damage-reduction in different trees…?"

"Probably because Stout is intended to work for weapon guarding rather than with shields?" Leafa suggested. "If you can block an attack without losing your stance, you can counterattack that much faster."

I nodded. "So the Brawn tree isn't just pure offense, either… Maybe I should take that one, too, then…"

"Can't you just take two of them?" Lisbeth asked.

"Mmm, I could," I admitted, "but it's always the case that if you master a single tree rather than spreading the points around, you end up tougher in the end."

Brawn
Bone-
breaker
Stout
Swiftness
Toughnes
Gallop
Perseverance
Dexterous
Anti-
venor
Sagacity
Concentration
Learned

"In that case, you should go for pure offense. That's the most like your style, anyway," Liz said. Leafa grinned for some reason, and Yui nodded with a big smile. I wanted to protest that I wasn't a *pure* damage dealer in *SAO* or *ALO*, but all three of them seemed on the same page, and I doubted that Asuna, Silica, or Alice would argue with it, either.

"...All right, but you guys are in support roles, then."

"Sure thing. We'll watch your back," Liz reassured me.

I touched the BRAWN icon again and then pressed the ACQUIRE button at the bottom of the pop-up window. Another dialog box appeared, asking if I wanted to expend an ability point. When I pressed the YES button, the window flashed with a jingling sound, and the black-and-white BRAWN icon turned red.

That made Bonebreaker and Stout available, but each of them cost two ability points this time. It seemed that each ability had ten ranks, so I had the option of taking Brawn all the way to rank-10 before I took Bonebreaker, if I wanted. I had eleven points left, but I didn't think I wanted to spend all of them yet.

After a bit of thinking, I went ahead and took Bonebreaker. That caused two more abilities to appear past it.

One was Assault, which provided a bonus to additional strikes during consecutive attacks. The other was Expand, which increased the span of area attacks. As I suspected, each took three points to unlock. In other words, getting to rank-10 in Brawn, Bonebreaker, and Assault altogether would take a total of sixty ability points. And there were probably more abilities farther up the tree.

"Boy, this is gonna take a while...," I muttered to myself, raising Brawn to rank-5. That meant I'd used seven points, leaving me with five more. I went back to my status screen, which showed the effect of Brawn now. The meters displaying my current usage of the total equipment weight and carry weight were a much lower percentage. There was a lot of water, food, and materials to carry around in this game, so it was a good bonus to have, even if it was boring.

"...Okay, I've got my abilities," I announced, closing the window.

"How many points did you leave?" Liz asked casually.

"Five, I think?"

"*Aha!* At least five! I win the bet!"

"...Huh?" I gaped.

Liz thrust her hand out toward Leafa, palm up. Leafa then poured a pile of nuts into her open hand. They'd made a bet about how many points I was going to leave unspent?

"Thanks a lot, Big Brother! What's the point of saving up your points? Be a man and make good use of them!" my little sister snapped, which seemed quite unfair to me.

Yui rubbed my head in consolation.

Done with our meal break, we hopped down to the ground from our impromptu safe zone atop the large boulder. Off to the southwest we continued, eschewing any man-made light to walk by the weak light of the stars.

We'd left the forest behind long ago; now there was nothing but dried grassland around. Because it was night, the monsters we encountered were nocturnal types, like hyenas and bats. They weren't pushovers, but they weren't too hard, either. That was thanks to Liz's metal equipment, of course—I'd have felt nervous about even leaving the woods with just the stone knife and ubiquigrass clothing.

For drinking water, Asuna filled up some handmade pottery canteens from the river, and we brought a bit of bear jerky to eat, but for the most part, we'd need to rustle up some supplies along the way. The hyenas' meat was inedible, even after being cooked, but now and then we found some short, rounded trees with walnut-like nuts. They were tough to crack but tasted good once you got them out. Two hours had passed since we left, but we were keeping TP and SP at around 80 percent so far.

"Liz, how far to the Bashin village?" I asked Lisbeth, who was walking with her map window open.

Over her shoulder, the blacksmith replied, "We're still only a third of the way there. There are two huge trees up ahead, and that's basically the halfway point, I'd say."

"Like how big? As big as the World Tree in Alfheim?" Leafa asked.

Lisbeth just grimaced and shook her head. "No, not *that* big. I'm not totally sure, because the last time we saw them was also at night, but I'd guess they're like three hundred feet?"

"That reminds me... When the Bashin passed a hill with a view of those big trees, they stopped to pray," added Yui, who was walking hand in hand with me.

"Oh, right! They did!" Lisbeth agreed.

"...Praying to the huge trees...," I repeated, thinking hard. Somehow, that imagery stimulated something deep in my memory, but I couldn't tell what it was summoning. I considered asking Yui to run that idea through her VRMMO database but thought better of it. Yui was another player now, not a navigation pixie, and what's more, she was excited about that. It wouldn't be fair of me to continue treating her like a convenient AI tool.

Instead, I was going to ask them if they'd stopped and prayed with the Bashin, but I got distracted by a cold, damp breeze from the north.

"Brrr. The night here is chilly for being a savanna... Aren't you cold, Yui?"

"No, I'm fine. Liz made armor for me, after all."

Indeed, Yui was no longer clad only in that little white dress; now she had on a thin breastplate, plus gloves and boots in the same design. She still wore the dress underneath these items, so it didn't look that warm. But Lisbeth's Blacksmithing skill proficiency was at 100, so even reduced from before, that was very high. Maybe she had worked a bonus against cold in there.

As for Lisbeth, she was still using the leather armor and one-handed mace the Bashin gave her, and out of the ingots cast from Blárkveld, she'd only made a small round shield for herself. Leafa, in contrast, had four pieces of metal equipment, same as me, including a long katana that could be used in one or both hands. Compared to our original stone gear, we'd transformed into a heavily armed combat force. But despite all that, Leafa shivered and complained the moment the northern wind hit us.

She turned back, whipping her golden ponytail behind her, and nimbly walked backward to talk face-to-face. "Hey, Kirito, can you make a cloak or something out of those hyena pelts?"

"Don't be silly. I don't even have the Tailoring skill."

"Then let's run! It'll make the trip go faster, too!"

"Uhhh...You might be able to run continuously because you get exercise in your school club, but I just go home after school..."

"You know that doesn't matter in the virtual world!" Leafa snapped.

I realized my mistake and cleared my throat to hide my embarrassment. "A-anyway, running is just a waste of TP and SP. And we can't see the ground very well, so it's dangerous..."

"But, Papa, we have torches!" Yui cried and removed a stick-like object from her inventory. It looked like a tree branch with some dried grass wrapped around the tip. The lights we used at the cabin were just dead branches, so this was a step beyond that.

"Did you make that, Yui?"

"Yes, but it was Liz's idea."

"Ooh, that's a professional crafter for you."

"I'm not paying out for compliments," Lisbeth remarked, glancing over her shoulder. "But...we should probably be ready to run soon. Last night the Bashin told us that the...Giyoru Savanna, was it? It sometimes has ice storms, and when that happens, you either need to wrap up with furs or find a cave. Otherwise, you'll die."

"What?! Why didn't you tell me that earlier?!"

"Because they said it only happens once every few years."

"Okay, you of all people should know that in a video game, that means once every few *days*...," I snapped.

But Yui, in a tiny, dejected voice, said, "I'm sorry, Papa. I heard them say it, too, but I did not classify it as important information."

"I—I'm not blaming you, Yui. I mean, who ever heard of ice storms on a savanna?"

"Hang on! What's with the difference in treatment here?!" Lisbeth fumed, puffing out her cheeks.

Just then, there was a gust from the north again, and the four of us hunched over simultaneously. It felt much colder than the previous one—and slightly wetter. I looked at the sky and saw black clouds rushing from north to south with great speed.

"...I'm getting a bad feeling about this," Leafa murmured. I offered a vote of agreement and looked down at Yui. "Let's get that torch lit."

"All right."

Yui solemnly pointed the grass-wrapped end of the branch toward me. I took a pair of flintstones out of my bag and struck them together. In the real world, flint had to be struck against a piece of metal called a firesteel to create sparks, but here, you just needed two stones. I struck them together, telling myself that even if I didn't take the Sagacity ability tree, I was going to learn the fire magic skill someday. On the seventh strike, the sparks landed true and began to burn the dried grass.

I put the flintstones back in my bag and took the torch from Yui, holding it high. The strong wind buffeted the flame, but it wasn't going to go out that easily.

A quick survey around us did not reveal any likely places to find a cave; if there was one nearby, the light wasn't strong enough to reach it. But it did show us a tall, narrow silhouette like a rock formation to the east and some gentle hill slopes to the west. Which way to go?

It wasn't a sure thing yet that an ice storm was going to sweep over us, but if we waited until then to search for shelter, it would already be too late. If there was a cave nearby, it would have to be at the rock formation, but it was shaped like a spire, so any potential hollowed-out caves were unlikely to be deep enough for us.

To my right, Yui cried out, "Something's coming from the north, Papa!"

"Huh…?"

I spun around, pointing the torch upwind, just as a huge, silent shadow slid into the range of the light.

Pausing just five yards away, the shadow stayed low to the ground and growled. This was not one of the hyenas we'd fought several times already. The black-furred body was slender but far bigger than a hyena's, and its front legs were burly by comparison. It wasn't a canine type but a feline…Based on the rounded ears, it was probably some kind of leopard.

"*Graaar!!*" the black panther roared, its light-blue eyes watching the four of us closely.

Why now?! I lamented. We couldn't run fast enough to get away from it, and it was clearly feeling hostile toward the torch. I moved the torch to my left hand and grabbed the handle of my sword.

"We're going to fight!" I shouted.

Leafa drew her weapon and stepped forward. Liz loosened her mace from its fasteners. I whispered "Take care of Yui" to her, and she replied, "Don't worry. I've got her."

Upon seeing my longsword and Leafa's katana, the panther bared its vicious fangs. They weren't as big as a saber-toothed tiger's, but they were at least three times as long as any real leopard's. Its pelt was dark as night, with a blue luster that ran from its neck down its spine.

The black panther crouched lower, entering a leaping stance. It was targeting me. I held my sword at my right shoulder, preparing to fight back with a sword skill.

Then there was an earsplitting roar—not from the panther but from the wind.

A gust that made all the previous bursts of wind seem cute by comparison blasted us. I had to tense my feet against the ground. Our valiant little torch couldn't withstand this and finally went out, plunging us into darkness. Hard pellets lashed my exposed face and hands. It was ice…hail.

Oh, hail no! I thought, although I didn't think anyone would have appreciated the wordplay because, just then, the panther leaped.

I started to activate the sword skill Vertical on instinct but stopped myself before I could plant my feet, and I spun around.

With incredible power, the panther jumped over all four of us, landing on the other side. It wasn't targeting us. It just ran farther south.

"Um, do you think...it was just running away from the storm...?" Liz wondered, just as the same thought occurred to me. If we were right, then these icy gusts were merely the warning blast of a storm so dangerous that even monsters fled from its path. It also meant the black panther had an evacuation destination in mind.

"Let's go after it!" I shouted, sheathing my sword and grabbing Yui's hand. We took off running, Lisbeth and Leafa close behind. The panther's silhouette blended into the darkness, and if it got more than a few yards away, we'd lose sight of it.

The torch was extinguished, so we couldn't see the ground. If any of us tripped on a change in elevation or a stone, that was it for our chase. I could only pray for real, actual luck during the pursuit. I considered scooping up Yui to carry her, but as a player, her agility was bound to be close to my own, and she was keeping up well.

For two minutes, we pursued the fleeing black panther. A small hill appeared up ahead. The panther leaped toward the foot of the hill, then seemingly vanished into it. When we arrived a moment later, there was a cave mouth about three feet tall, dark against the hillside.

As soon as I stopped, hail struck my iron armor from behind, clanging off the metal. The pellets were only a fraction of an inch in size now, but they were bound to get worse. The temperature was dropping, too; my breath was turning white.

I could also see that my HP bar was dropping, bit by bit. A blinking Debuff icon shaped like an ice crystal at the right end of the bar told me all I needed to know.

"Papa, let's go inside!" Yui urged. I nodded. The cave went much farther in, and we just had to pray that the panther had gone as far as it could.

I let go of Yui's hand and drew my sword just in case as I approached the cave mouth. I couldn't see anything inside. The wind was so strong that no torch would last more than a second at this point. I steeled my nerves and bent down to go inside.

The cave sloped gently downward, and the ceiling got higher as I proceeded. The cave was small at the ground level, but it seemed that the full dimensions expanded as it went down. I continued onward, feeling a bit relieved about that.

After about thirty feet, the slope leveled out, and I stopped moving forward and straightened up. The ceiling was high enough that I could reach upward with my sword and not touch anything. It was quite a large space, then. There was no sign of the black panther.

I checked on my HP bar, which had stopped decreasing and no longer had a freezing Debuff icon. I exhaled and turned back around. The cave was pitch-black, with almost no visibility.

"Are you all here?" I whispered.

"Yes, Papa." "I'm here." "Sure am!"

Relieved, I started to put my sword back so that we could light the torch again. But then I heard Leafa gasp "Wh-what's that…?" and spun around.

I still couldn't see a thing. But after squinting long enough, I got a message that said *Night Vision skill gained. Proficiency has risen to 1.* And just like that, it became a tiny bit easier to see in the dark.

And soon, I noticed it, too.

In the depths of the cave floated two blue lights. *What is that?* I wondered. They went out, then lit again. Almost like a blink…

No. It *was* a blink. The eyes of the panther that had come in before us.

We'd been noticed.

"Grrrr…"

The beast growled, and the blue eyes rose higher, suggesting that the panther went from lying on its side to a standing position. Obviously, its night vision was far better than ours, so if this turned into a fight, we didn't stand a chance.

"Yui, light the torch," I murmured, holding the torch in my left hand behind my back.

"Okay," she replied and took it. I was going to hand her the flintstones, but before I could, there was a strange sound.

It was a high-pitched creaking, something that did not sound like it came from the panther. Wary of the enemy ahead of us, I quickly spun around and saw that tiny white particles were sweeping in from the mouth of the cave.

The moment the particles touched Lisbeth, who was the farthest back, she sneezed loudly. Leafa shrieked, "It's cold!" and Yui moaned. Lastly, I shivered. It was worse than just *cold.* The freezing Debuff icon was there again, and I could see my HP dropping. We couldn't avoid the chill from the mouth of the cave at this location. I could even hear the whistling of the wind, which sounded like faint screaming. I didn't want to imagine what it was like out in the open.

"Big Brother, we have to go farther in!" Leafa urged nervously. I shouted back "I know, but what about the panther?!" The monster in the back of the cave wasn't attacking, but it continued to growl. It wasn't hard to imagine the beast pouncing on us if we got any closer.

My HP bar had dropped 10 percent. At this rate, it would hit zero in less than three minutes. I supposed that we'd just have to fight the panther, regardless of the disadvantages...but then I remembered something we could still try out.

I dropped my sword back into my sheath and stuck my hand into my tool bag, then removed a thin, flat object. It was the bear jerky Asuna had made for us. The emergency ration was important, but I'd never need to eat it if I died from the cold or the panther.

"C'mon, it's yummy! It's dinner!" I called out to the blue eyes in the darkness and tossed the dried meat. It fell to the ground, attracting the attention of the panther. It blinked. Then blinked again.

The blue eyes silently moved toward the meat. I sensed the panther sniffing at the air. After several tense seconds, I heard a creaking sound. The black panther had bitten the jerky. Instantly, there was a glowing ring in the darkness, looking like a car speedometer. Around one third of it was full from the lower left and colored red, while the end of it jittered up and down. That was the beast-taming meter Asuna said appeared when she was catching Aga.

I pulled out another piece of jerky, my last, and tossed it forward. The panther immediately grabbed it, and the meter rose another 10 percent.

"Give me your jerky."

I reached behind my back, and Yui promptly dropped a piece of meat into my palm. Trying to sense when the panther was done eating, I hurled the third stick of jerky. The meter went up farther to the halfway point. The first piece of jerky put it at 30 percent, and the next two added 10 percent each. Yui should have one piece of jerky, plus two each from Liz and Leafa, which should give us just enough.

Trusting in my calculation, I continued tossing the dried meat to the panther. For each bit of the beast-taming meter we pushed upward, our HP dropped. At level-13, I had more overall HP than the others, who were only around level-4 or level-5. I could see on the party readout below my own HP bar that their health was already under the halfway point.

Hurry, hurry, I prayed. But I had a feeling that the timing of food lures was the key to beast-taming success in this game: Wait for the monster to finish eating so that the meter was rising when you gave it the next piece of food. Any faster or slower, and it wouldn't work.

Once I had given the panther the second piece of Yui's jerky, then both of Liz's, the beast-taming meter was about 80 percent full. Asuna had given Aga three pieces of bear meat to tame it, so this panther was much harder. Either it was because we were giving it dried meat rather than fresh or because the panther was a much higher level.

"Leafa."

"Okay."

She placed the ninth piece of meat in my palm, and I tossed it. The panther gobbled it up, taking the meter to 90 percent.

"Leafa."

"That's all."

"……Huh?"

I spun around to face my little sister, whose silhouette I could only just barely make out in the darkness. "What do you mean, that's all? Asuna gave us three pieces each! And we each ate one when we stopped for a break, so we should all have two…"

"I ate two, actually."

"Huh?!"

"I couldn't help it! I was hungry!"

"Wha…?"

I was aghast, but what was gone was gone. It was too late to get back all the hyena meat we left behind, too. I had a feeling the panther wouldn't eat that hideous-smelling stuff anyway.

The panther's beast-taming meter was now wavering around 90 percent. If we did nothing and it started to drop, all of our effort and supplies would have amounted to nothing.

I heard Yui whimper, "Papa…my HP…"

"Yui," I murmured, dropping the unlit torch and pulling my daughter closer so I could wrap my arms around her. Even through her armor, I could tell that her body was freezing cold and trembling. Her HP bar was down to barely over 10 percent at this point. I couldn't just let her freeze to death.

My mind was made up. I inched forward, holding Yui. Getting farther away from the entrance eased the cold, but the black panther started to growl again. The beast-taming meter, still wavering, started to shift into a negative trend.

There was no food left to give. But food couldn't be the only way to lift that meter.

"You don't have to be afraid...I'm not your enemy," I whispered to the beast as I approached. The panther's growling got louder, but it was neither fleeing nor attacking for now.

I closed within six feet...three feet...two feet. At this distance, I could finally see the creature's outline. Its head was low, ready to pounce at any moment. The beast-taming meter was down to 80 percent.

Ready for it to be bitten off, I extended my hand. When I touched the powerful neck of the panther, its body jolted.

"There you go. Good boy..."

I brushed its luxurious fur with my fingertips. The growling did not stop. The meter was still dropping, bit by bit. But if I showed any fear now, the panther was sure to attack right away. I continued to stroke it with my right hand, holding Yui in my left. The panther's muscles tensed, relaxed, then tensed again.

"Grrr...rrrrr..."

As the growling got lower, the panther's head followed. Was it a sign of impending attack or something else?

"Rrrr...grorrr..."

The constant rumbling in the giant cat's throat had changed somewhat. It was more of a rolling sound now, like a giant version of a cat purring.

At last, its powerful neck muscles relaxed, and the beast-taming meter stopped descending and began to rise once again. The black panther rolled onto its side and allowed me to pet it. The meter hit 80 percent and then went past 90.

"There you go...Good boy...," I whispered, reaching back with my other hand. Leafa had seen Aga get tamed and knew to hand me a rope of ubiquigrass.

Annoyingly slowly, the beast-taming meter finally reached its full length, and that was when I looped the end of the grass around the panther's neck to form a circle. With tense fingers, I closed it tight, and the big cat's body flashed, summoning a green circle

over its head. Underneath the ring-shaped HP bar was the species name: *Lapispine Dark Panther.* There was also a message for me: *Domestication skill gained. Proficiency has risen to 1.*

So it's a dark panther, rather than a black panther. Okay. But what does lapispine *mean?* I wondered, though there was no time for that now. I shouted "Huddle around the panther!" to Leafa and Lisbeth, and pressed Yui against the neck of the beast. The other girls draped themselves over the thick, soft fur on its stomach.

The cat's body temperature was high, and the warmth bloomed through my near-freezing skin. I exhaled with relief. My HP stopped dropping, and the freezing Debuff icon disappeared. The icy particles were still streaming in from the entrance, but they didn't reach the back of this little cave.

Feeling secure at last, I asked a question to no one in particular.

"...What does *lapispine* mean? Like *intestine*?"

Leafa rubbed at the bluish part of the panther's back and replied, "Probably because of this lapis-blue patch on its spine, right?"

"Oh...lapis spine..."

Lisbeth asked, "So what are we calling it?"

"Hmm? Well...it's black, so it should be Kuro," I said after two quick seconds of consideration. Leafa and Liz cried out "That's so boring!" in unison. But Yui said, "It's simple and good." I decided to ask the creature in question.

"It's a good name, right, Kuro?"

The black panther barked, "*Graar!*"

7

"...I knew I should have asked..."

Sinon lifted the end of the pelt she had wrapped around her body to look outside.

What had been dry grassland just minutes ago was now a field of pure white. She reached out and scooped up some of the white stuff, letting the fine particles trickle between her fingers. It was piled-up hail pellets, not snow.

When Fikki the Ornith girl had given her this pelt cloak, she'd said, *If a אא comes, use it.* The word Sinon couldn't make out because of her lack of language proficiency was probably something like *hailstorm*. Or maybe it was *blizzard from hell.* It certainly felt like one when it swept over. She'd dived into a little hollow beneath a boulder and wrapped herself tight in the pelt cloak, but even then, it'd taken away nearly half her HP bar.

Once she'd confirmed that the freezing Debuff icon didn't activate when she took off the cloak, Sinon emerged from under the rock. She now stared in wonder at the world of silvery-white around her, reflecting the light of the moon.

She'd run as much as she could in the hour since leaving the Ornith village and probably covered twelve miles before the hailstorm arrived. Looking at how much hail was covering the earth all the way to the horizon, she was worried for the village. There was no turning back now, however. She didn't know how many miles it was to the Bashin village, but if she didn't get there tonight, she'd have to log out in the middle of the wide-open Giyoru Savanna. The current situation in *Unital Ring* was the biggest emergency in the VR gaming world since the *SAO* Incident in 2022, but Sinon wasn't bold enough to use that as an excuse to skip school.

She sat down again at the foot of the rock, resisting the urge to go on the move again. The pelt went back into her inventory, replaced by Fikki's hard bread. It was indeed teeth-breakingly hard, and it didn't have much flavor, but she put up with it because she didn't have time to start a fire. Her HP and SP slowly began to recover. Once she got her HP up to about 80 percent, she drank from her canteen. She'd used up quite a lot with all the running, so she needed to look for fresh water soon…

"…Oh! Unless…"

She scooped up some of the nearly infinite supply of hailstones and trickled them into the canteen. After a moment, the ice melted, and the level refilled a bit. After a couple repetitions, the container was full again. The temperature was rising, too, so the hail on the ground would melt soon. As long as she had a container, she could refill as much water as she wanted. But of course, there were no canteens or water jugs just lying around on the ground, and Sinon had neither the materials nor the necessary skill to make one.

Sinon examined the details of the Ornith canteen closely. It seemed to be made of waterproof leather. Though she hadn't thought about it before, it occurred to her now that the light and sturdy canteen was probably more valuable than the life-giving water inside it. Between the muskets and the contemporary-looking buildings, the Orniths seemed to have quite an advanced civilization. Too bad she wasn't likely to visit them again for quite a while.

For now, she drank from the freshly chilled water to refill her TP bar, then sloshed more hail into the canteen to top it off. If she ran quickly, she could probably use it up and refill it one more time before all the ice melted.

Sinon picked up the musket from the side of the boulder, slung it over her back, checked that her laser gun was still on her hip, then began sprinting across the silvery plains.

Out of the fifteen ability points she had acquired, Sinon spent ten to take the Swiftness ability and its two offshoots, Gallop and Dexterous. From Swiftness, that gave her a bonus to ranged-weapon damage, small-melee-weapon damage, and jumping distance; from Gallop, reduced rate of SP and TP decrease when running; and from Dexterous, a bonus to ranged-weapon accuracy and lock-picking change. She was curious about the offshoots of Gallop, Sprint, and Acrobat, and the offshoots of Dexterous, Vital Aim, and Adroit, but she held off for now because the third-tier abilities cost three points each. Saving five points was probably more cautious than she needed to be, but she had a feeling she'd soon want abilities from outside the Swiftness tree—particularly from the Toughness tree.

For now, the effect of the lower TP/SP cost from Gallop was huge. At just rank-2, she could already tell that they were draining slower. She couldn't have run twelve miles in an hour without it.

Sinon ran persistently, eager to make up the time she'd lost because of the storm. Before now, she'd had to avoid monsters as well as their likely hiding places. But now that the storm had passed, it seemed as though all the creatures had burrowed underground, because she couldn't see a single moving thing anymore as she hurried southeast. Eight inches of hail on the ground made for a crunchy surface underfoot, but unlike snow, it was tightly packed and did not slow her down.

After fifteen minutes, the ice began to thaw. It was melting as the temperature rose again. She stopped, drank from her water supply to refill her TP, then scooped up more ice. More of it was melting even as she did this, so the next time she drank, she'd need to find a new source to fill up her water. Hopefully, that'd be *after* she was out of the savanna.

Up ahead near the horizon, lit by dim starlight now that the clouds had blown past, she could see the dark outline of mountains…or a cliff. She'd crossed eighteen miles of the flat expanse, and up ahead it was split with a giant wall of a cliff.

Was that the end of the plains? Did that mean the Bashin village was close to the wall?

With hope in her heart, Sinon gazed at the foot of the cliff from north to south. But at no point did she see any sign of man-made light. It was a bit before nine PM, which seemed early for lights in a village to be out, but she had to have faith.

The ice was melting all around her now, returning the grassland to its regular state. The beasts and insects that had burrowed to get away from the chill would be active again soon. She reminded herself that she'd need to be wary of monsters once more, and she continued her run.

As she got closer, the scale of the cliff was far bigger than she realized.

It was easily over 150 feet tall and almost entirely vertical, so climbing it was out of the question. She couldn't tell whether to go north or south around it because there was no way to tell which side of it ended sooner.

Sinon had never seen them for herself, but in the Underworld, there were giant barriers called the Everlasting Walls, which split the four empires into separate territories, and not even the nobles or emperors themselves could cross them. That kind of absurdity existed because it was a simulation, not a game. And because *Unital Ring* was a game, there had to be some way to get through this wall.

She looked around and found a large rock with a flat top, which she climbed for a better vantage. Once she was sure there were no monsters around, she opened her inventory and materialized the Hecate II.

Sinon knew it was pointless, but just to be sure, she tried to lift the heavy antimateriel gun. It would not budge. Even though Sinon was level-16, it was over her Equip Weight limit. She sighed, then got down and peered through the scope. She could pull it off the gun and use it as a mini-telescope by hand, if she wanted, but then she'd have to realign and adjust it again after reattaching it. The process was much easier in virtual reality than in the real world, from what she'd read, but you also needed to do a test fire to confirm it was right, and that was a waste.

So she painfully realigned the Hecate's direction until she could look through the scope for a better view of the wall. The blackish surface was so smooth that it didn't even look natural. Free-climbing that wall would be suicide. There were little trees growing here and there out of the surface, but there were not nearly enough of them to climb all the way up. Examining the northern side of the wall turned up nothing more of interest, so she slowly spun the Hecate on its bipod to point the other way, to the south, and looked through the scope again.

"Ah..."

She zoomed in on the scope. There was a slope carved into the wall at one point, like a set of stairs. Following the trail, feeling her heart beating in her throat, she saw it vanish at the top into a tunnel, its mouth black and yawning.

There was an unpleasant mixture of excitement at finding the passage through the cliff wall and anxiety about heading through a tight area, the bane of all snipers. In any case, she had no other options. The Hecate went back into her inventory. Sinon stood up; her HP was full again, thanks to the hard bread, and her TP and SP were almost 90 percent full. She wished she could put some of that perpetually full MP to practice use, but for now, she had no idea how to gain any magic skills.

She still had her Sniper Rifle Mastery skill from *GGO*. What if she could become not a magic swordsman—but a magic gunman? That would be cool.

With that enticing thought in mind, Sinon resumed running toward the titanic wall.

8

The sight of the pale moonlight shining down upon the white, ice-crusted plains was so beautiful that I was left speechless, even knowing it was all just a virtual rendering. It was our newest party member, Kuro, the lapispine dark panther, who brought me back to reality with a headbutt to my waist.

"*Rrrr...*," it purred, telling me to get going. I gave its neck a scratch and replied "Good idea. We're almost to the Bashin village."

In fact, the village wasn't our final destination. We were going to ask them for information about the birdpeople Sinon had met, and then we'd have to continue from there. If we could meet up with Sinon by midnight, that was probably the best outcome we could hope for.

Thanks to the hailstorm, the little monsters were out of the way, so it was best if we ran as far as we could while the coast was clear. I was about to give the signal to launch when Lisbeth cut me off.

"About that, Kirito."

"About what...the Bashin?"

"Yeah. Remember how I said Silica, Yui, and I had a meal in the Bashin's big tent? Well...they had a bunch of fur rugs on the ground in there."

"And…?"

"I'm pretty sure I saw one of them that was a mixture of black and blue…"

"…"

I looked away from Liz to Kuro's back. The shining black fur had a streak of brilliant blue running down its spine, just as the species name described.

Yui was already enamored with Kuro. She patted its back and added, "Yes, there was a rug in the corner of the tent with this color arrangement on it. It was a ninety-nine percent match with Kuro's fur."

If Yui said it, then mistaken memory wasn't a factor. That left no doubt that the Bashin hunted lapispine dark panthers on the savanna.

True or not, in a normal game, an NPC would never attack a player's tamed monster. Still, there was no guarantee it would work the same way in *Unital Ring.*

"Hmm. In that case, what if we have you wait with Kuro outside the village so that we can go and collect information inside?" Leafa suggested. That was a logical idea, and I was going to add that they should get some food for me, too, if they got fed.

But then Yui spoke again. "Actually, Papa, we might not need to go into the village at all."

"Huh? What do you mean?"

"The earlier storm was of considerable scope. If Sinon encountered the same storm, it's possible she could be on the opposite side of the savanna."

"…I see. That's true…But how will we make contact with Sinon, then? She's not a registered friend or party member, so we can't send messages," I said.

Yui beamed. "Why do you need to contact her in *Unital Ring*? Why not in the real world?"

Following my daughter's advice, I logged out and sat upright. Going from the icy white plains to my man-made room gave me a bout of momentary dizziness until I looked to my side. On the left side of the bed was Suguha, wearing her AmuSphere and looking defenseless in her sleep...but of course, she wasn't sleeping. Suguha was currently in a far-off virtual world, protecting my avatar. We knew there were no enemies in visible range, but there was always the possibility of a dangerous monster popping into existence, so I needed to hurry.

I lifted the AmuSphere visor and grabbed my phone. With the introduction of the Augma, it was quickly becoming an obsolete bit of gadgetry, but I used it to call Sinon anyway.

She was probably in the midst of a *UR* dive, too, but the AmuSphere had a linking feature to your smartphone that allowed you to receive calls there. Assuming she had it turned on—and that she wasn't in the midst of battle or something else just as important—she should answer. I waited patiently for thirty seconds, listening to the ring signal.

"*Make it quick!*" came her response, getting right to the point. That was Sinon's voice, so I obliged her request by launching into the topic at hand.

"Did you get stuck in the ice storm?!"

"Nearly froze to death about twenty minutes ago."

"So you're in the Giyoru Savanna, too?"

"Yes, I'm heading southeast from the northwest."

"Got it. We'll head northwest from the southeast! Is there any terrain near you that makes for a good landmark?"

"You bet there is. There's a gigantic natural wall running north to south, probably through the middle of the savanna. I went into a cave through the wall. That's where I am right now."

"Cave in the wall...? Any monsters?"

"Tons. I logged out in a safe-ish place, but they could pop up at any time, so I can't stick around."

She was doing the exact same thing I was, but while I had my teammates and pet to protect me, Sinon was all alone. If she got attacked while she was logged-out, she'd die in moments.

"All right. We'll go into the wall from the east side. Just hang in there."

"Got it. Thanks."

She hung up. I took a quick sip of water, then lay down on the bed again and lowered the AmuSphere visor.

Back on the moonlit plains, the ice had begun to melt in the few minutes I'd been logged-out. The girls scooped up the remaining ice and drained it into the water jugs. No monsters had appeared in the area yet.

"I'm back!" I called out, rising to my feet. Kuro rubbed its head on me again. Despite its fierce appearance, it seemed to be very cuddly once it took to you. After feeding it all the bear jerky, we'd need to find some more food soon.

Lisbeth, Leafa, and Yui gathered around to listen to Sinon's message.

"A natural wall…?" Leafa murmured, staring to the northwest. I did the same, but there was nothing visible beyond the darkness of the horizon. I started to worry that there was some huge misunderstanding afoot. But Sinon had risked her character's life to pass on that information, so I just had to trust it.

"Let's hurry," I said. The girls nodded, and Kuro issued a quick chuff.

We ran across the plains, encountering two packs of the familiar hyenas and one bison-like monster. The bison was a bit of a handful, but with Kuro distracting the beast and performing acrobatic feats, we were free to use enough sword skills to whittle down its HP. The rest of the girls each earned a level from that fight.

The bison also dropped a ton of raw meat, which Kuro was very happy to eat, thankfully. Now I wouldn't have to worry for a while about the tamed effect wearing off due to hunger.

There were no more encounters after that point. Thirty minutes of travel later, Yui pointed ahead and shouted, "I can see a wall!"

I stopped and squinted until a surface rising directly above the plains was visible to me. The massive cliff ran from north to south, and its scale reminded me of the Everlasting Walls from the Underworld.

"And somewhere in there is a cave where Sinon's waiting?" asked Lisbeth. That was correct, but the more I thought about it, the tougher it was going to be to find one little cave mouth on a surface that was miles long. Plus, there was no guarantee that there'd be only *one* of them. I thought hard, trying not to panic about the task ahead.

"...Papa, this might not be fair, but I'm going to enhance my eyesight to look for the cave," Yui announced, her eyes wide.

Of the four of us, Lisbeth, Leafa, and I were using our brains to "see" the visual information the AmuSphere provided, but as an AI, Yui could process the brightness and contrast of those details all she wanted. I didn't want to treat her like some kind of convenient software tool, but we *had* to meet up with Sinon. Besides, if we'd proceeded to the Bashin village like we'd originally planned, I'd be asking her to interpret for us there anyway. One way or another, I needed Yui's help.

"I'd appreciate that," I murmured. Yui briefly looked at me, smiled, then turned back to concentrate. A few seconds later, she pointed at a spot ahead of us.

"I've found it! There's a staircase and a cave entrance in this direction!"

"Thanks, Yui!" said Leafa, hugging the little girl. Liz rubbed her head, too.

From here, there was no way to tell how thick across the cliff wall was, but I couldn't imagine it being miles long. Even if the cave made a dungeon, it wouldn't be that big.

Hang in there just a bit longer, Sinon! I told her silently and started running in the direction that Yui pointed.

The faint cliff off in the distance grew more and more substantial as we approached, and once we were at its foot, the size of it left us speechless. The cliff was about 150 feet tall, and though there were wider elevation gaps in Alfheim, the distance this wall covered was vast. A single line of vertical cliff that stretched from one end of the horizon to the other was the sort of thing that typically looked like lazy level-design in a game, but for some reason, in the world of *Unital Ring*, it felt like a true natural wonder.

The dark rock face was hard and smooth; there was no way to climb it by hand. Perhaps it might be possible to craft a ladder to place against it, but there were no trees or vines nearby to harvest for material. We'd have to use the stairs Yui'd spotted.

Those stairs were carved out of just a foot of space along the cliff face, with nothing to hold on to. It was close to a hundred feet to get to the cave entrance, so one bad misstep would mean certain death. I wanted to place a guide rope on the wall, but over an hour had passed since I contacted Sinon, and we couldn't keep her waiting any longer.

"Kuro, can you get up these stairs?" I asked. The black panther growled, then hopped ten feet up the steps without fear. It even wagged its tail with excitement.

Well, it wouldn't do for its master to be afraid of the challenge now.

"Okay...here I go," I announced. Behind me, Lisbeth huffed "Come on—hurry up already."

Thankfully, we reached the top without any accidents, but we didn't dare relax until we were all inside the open mouth of the cave at the end. The stairs were man-made, so I figured the cave was, too, but it seemed to be natural. Meaning someone had carved out the steps from the cliff in order to reach the hole yawning in the middle of the wall. That would have been an NPC, not a player, of course. But was it these Bashin people or someone else? There was no way to know.

In any case, this was the first proper dungeon to explore since our forced conversion yesterday. I doubted any players had been in here before us, so any materials or treasure chests—if they existed—would be there for the taking. That made me want to chart out every step of the place, but meeting up with Sinon was our top priority.

We'd run a long way to get here, so my SP bar was below 60 percent, and my TP was below 50. We had plenty of drinking water, but the only food was raw bison meat. For now, I decided to drink some fluids and feed Kuro the meat and water, and we could eat something after finding Sinon.

"This is kind of an unorthodox party, so how are you thinking we'll take formation?" asked Leafa once she had put away her water jug.

I considered that and replied, "Me and Kuro in the front, Liz and Yui in the middle, and you take the rear, Leafa. Yui and I can hold the torches."

Lisbeth made a face like she wanted to say something. She was the only one with a shield, so she probably wanted to stand up front to play a tank, but I wanted her to focus more on protecting Yui. Thankfully, she took my point and didn't argue.

"Fine, just switch out as soon as things get hairy."

"Thanks. I'm counting on you."

And with that, we had our 2-2-1 formation.

Among VRMMO players, there was a tendency to think that there was plenty of time to assume formation once battle started, and lining up while you were only on the move was dumb and uncool. I'd probably agree with that ninety-nine times out of a hundred, but in Aincrad, it took only one moment of carelessness to lead to tragedy—especially in a dungeon, where things were cramped and chaotic. Even now that we weren't in a death game anymore, I tended to be thorough about battle formation.

"Tell me if you notice any monsters," I whispered to Kuro, scratching its neck. The panther answered "*Graar.*"

Sinon said there were "tons" of monsters over the phone, and that did not turn out to be an exaggeration. There were plenty of slimy amphibian-type monsters in the dank cave, and they had us constantly on our heels. Fortunately, Kuro's advanced searching capabilities enabled it to growl a warning before we saw our enemies, and we were able to fight back all of them easily. Even Yui showed off the fruits of her training with Alice. She fought bravely with her short sword, proving that I was a little *too* worried about her.

Onward we went through the cave, slaying giant newts, legless caecilians, and axolotls. Unfortunately, we didn't come across any treasure chests, but there were more than a few veins of iron and bronze ore, so we stocked up on everything we could find.

After twenty minutes, I was getting worried about my SP, but I didn't want to chow down on raw newt, either. From the rear, Leafa said, "It's kind of weird, don't you think?"

"What's weird?"

"We're dealing with all of these amphibians, and there are so many newts and salamanders, yet there hasn't been a single—"

Blaaaam!

There was a dry, distant echoing sound that came from farther in, causing Leafa to stop in the middle of her sentence.

I hadn't heard that particular sound once in this dungeon—or in *Unital Ring* at all. Kuro paused, twitching, and began to growl. That had to be a gunpowder explosion: a gunshot.

"It's Sinon!" I shouted, trying not to make too much noise, and looked over my shoulder. "Yui, can you tell which direction that came from?"

"I'm analyzing the echoes...It came from a hallway ahead and to the right!" she stated. I thanked her and picked up my pace. At the next fork, we went right and followed the tunnel as it curved and descended somewhat.

Suddenly, the cave widened ahead. We were near the top of a huge domed hollow. It had to be nearly fifty yards across. That was much farther than the torches were capable of illuminating, but I could see the overall size of the dome because of some kind of luminescent moss growing on the walls.

A narrow sloped path ran from our location along the wall to the floor of the dome. The floor was split between damp rocks and dark water, and atop a boulder in the middle was a human silhouette.

It wore a tight-fitting suit of armor and a white muffler. In its arms was something like a long stick—a gun. There couldn't be another gunner here by coincidence. We'd finally found her.

"Si—," I started to call out but swallowed the sound.

Behind the gunner were more humanoid shapes. But though they were upright, they were not human. Pointed snouts, big round ears…Their heads were clearly those of mice. They carried weapons that looked like pitchforks. Their narrow tails swayed as they advanced upon the gunner. There were two…no, three of them.

"Sinon, behind you!!" I called out, descending the steps on the side of the dome as fast as I could. Kuro and the others followed close behind me.

The gunner, Sinon, looked up and then behind her. There was no more than fifteen feet separating her from the ratmen. She could shoot one of them, but the other two would skewer her with their weapons.

"Ryaaa!"

I leaped halfway down the path into a shallow pool. The jump created a huge splash and took a few of my HP, but I didn't care. I pulled back, preparing to throw my torch at the closest ratman to Sinon.

"No, Kirito! They're not enemies!" I heard her shout, and I hastily adjusted my grip on the torch. The panther was about to leap on another one of them, so I told it, "Kuro, stop!"

The panther hit the brakes, and the three ratmen shrieked "אאאא!" and backed away toward the wall. There was another hallway mouth there, a different one from the way we'd come inside.

My eyes met Sinon's as she stood atop the boulder. She had light-blue hair that was slightly pointed at the ends, and sharp, catlike eyes—it was undoubtedly Sinon. But the rifle she was holding looked really old-fashioned and wasn't all that similar to her usual weapon, the PGM Ultima Ratio Hecate II. Assuming that the Hecate was over her Equip Weight limit, much like my Blárkveld and Excalibur, where did she get *this* gun? But it wasn't like that mattered now.

"If these ratmen aren't the enemy, then who are you fighting, Sinon?!" I demanded as Lisbeth, Yui, and Leafa reached the floor of the dome. Sinon's expression softened when she saw them splashing through the puddles, but it didn't last long.

"Get up out of the water, everyone!" she shouted. "Preferably atop tall rocks!"

Her tone brooked no argument, so I held my questions for later and started to clamber up a nearby boulder. But before I could get up, I heard a splash nearby.

Something was approaching under the water at tremendous speed. There was no time to avoid it; something hit my right ankle. I'd been bitten—no, grabbed?

Suddenly, my foot got wrenched aside, and I fell into the water. The torch flew out of my hand and fizzled out. With the sword in my right hand, I tried to sever the ropelike thing wrapped around my ankle, but I couldn't reach. It was going to drag me into the depths—

"*Growwr!*" Kuro snarled and plunged headfirst into the water, then emerged holding the thing that was pulling me in its fangs.

It was not a rope. It was some kind of slimy, pink tentacle thing.

"Big Brother!"

Leafa lifted her katana and activated Sonic Leap. *Shwa!* She split the surface of the water in two. It was a perfectly boosted attack, performed with great skill by her real-life expert swordsmanship. The glowing green blade struck the tentacle Kuro was pulling—but did not sever it.

Lisbeth's steel katana sank a few inches into the pink tentacle but stopped there. The rubbery appendage twanged and bounced back.

"Aaaah!" "*Grrarp?!*"

It threw Leafa and Kuro back together with a massive splash. But their attack paid off, because the tentacle let go of my ankle and sank back into the deeper water.

I helped Leafa up and got atop the rock for good this time. Yui and Lisbeth retreated to different rocks, and Kuro leaped up next to me in a single bound.

"What was that, Sinon?!" I gasped.

The gunner brandished her old-fashioned rifle and replied, "It'll pop out of the water soon! Keep your eyes peeled. It moves fast!"

No sooner had the words left her mouth than there was a loud splash, and a dark shape leaped out of the water on the distant side of the pool. It was large, about six feet long...and if its extremely long and powerful legs stretched out, it could uncurl to twice that length. The front legs, meanwhile, were weak and small, and its head was a part of its torso.

The gigantic creature leaped from puddle to puddle with dizzying speed, then landed and stuck to the wall of the dome. Lisbeth, Yui, Leafa, and I all cried the same word at the same time.

"Frog!!"

Aside from the size of it, everything about the monster was perfectly froggish. It had large, bulging eyes and a diamond-shaped torso. Its legs folded in the middle and ended in long, flared fingers that looked like suckers.

At last, I understood what Leafa was trying to say before we heard the gunshot. We had seen lots of newts and salamanders—but no *frogs*.

"Hey, lucky you. Here's the frog you wanted," I said, staring up at the signature amphibian stuck to the wall.

"I didn't *want* there to be frogs." Leafa pouted. "Especially gigantic ones..."

"That's got to be the boss of this cave..."

I wasn't just guessing about that. I'd taken a tentacle attack to my right leg, so I could see the ring cursor over the giant frog's head. Its individual name was *Goliath Rana*. All of the previous monsters we'd met, including Kuro, had descriptive Japanese names, but this one was in English, which I assumed had to mean something. Assuming it was actually English, of course.

"...*Goliath* means 'giant,' right? What's *rana*?" I murmured.

Yui replied, "I believe it's the name of the family of true frogs. In Japan, they're labeled as red frogs."

Sure enough, the body of the giant frog was dark red, and its eyes flickered like flames.

The Goliath Rana's bulging eyes blinked, and it began to climb the wall at a relaxed pace. The more it climbed and the steeper the negative angle became, the more eerily weightless it seemed, a cow-sized shape refusing to fall.

"Wouldn't this be the time to shoot it, Sinon?" I asked, realizing my suggestion was probably unwanted.

The gunner kept the rifle at her side without budging. She stared up at the frog and spat, "I've shot it several times already. But its back is too tough for these musket bullets to pierce."

Thanks to *The Three Musketeers* and such, I knew that muskets were an old-fashioned kind of gun. But you couldn't call them "rifles," because there wasn't any rifling on the inside of the barrels. This made me wonder where she'd gotten such a thing, but this wasn't the time to be asking irrelevant questions.

"...Can you manage to shoot the Hecate with extra help?" I wondered.

She shot me down at once. "Nope. We can't get the angle while it's on the ceiling, and when it's on the ground, it's moving too fast to aim at."

"Good point..."

I was still curious about the ratpeople behind us, but as long as they weren't hostile, I could find out the answer later. This was the time to figure out how to beat the Goliath Rana.

"Remember, Kirito, for most of the frog-type monsters in Aincrad, the weak point was the stomach," noted Lisbeth, holding her mace.

"Good point. Let's get it to expose its belly before attacking."

"But how?" asked Leafa.

"Ummm..."

Just then, the giant frog reached the very top of the hundred-foot-tall dome and looked down at us with its creepy eyes, completely upside-down.

"Here it comes!" Sinon shouted right as the frog's powerful legs launched it off the rock and straight at *me* with blinding speed.

"Aaaah!"

I did a backflip out of pure instinctual reaction to avoid the hit, but the rock I was standing on got obliterated, pelting my body with stone shards. I lost only 3 percent of my HP, but it would have been much worse if not for my metal armor. And without a single potion to use, any accumulation of damage would eventually prove fatal.

The others hadn't lost any HP, fortunately. But then I realized I was forgetting something important. I backed farther away, called up the ring menu, and hit the INVITE icon in the communication tab, then slid down to Sinon's name. She immediately accepted, adding a new abbreviated bar to the list in the upper left corner of my vision.

The Goliath Rana remained in place for about three seconds after its meteoric crash, then began to move again. It jumped into a nearby pool of water and vanished.

"On top of the rocks!" Sinon instructed, so we jumped onto nearby boulders again. Out of the corner of my eye, I caught sight of Yui and Kuro climbing up, then asked Sinon, "So its attack patterns are a dive into the water, followed by a tentacle attack, then climbing to the ceiling and diving down? Just those two?"

"For now. And that's its tongue, not a tentacle."

"Oh…that makes more sense."

So when the Goliath Rana grabbed my ankle, it wasn't trying to drown me but eat me. If I had only one life to live in *Unital Ring*, I was going to do everything in my power to avoid going out like *that*.

After enough time waiting atop the rocks, we lured the frog out of the water again, where it began to climb the wall. We didn't have an avenue to attack yet, but if we avoided the dive attack, at least we wouldn't take major damage…But that wasn't the right line of thought. Each one of its dives was destroying a safe rock to stand on, so we would eventually lose our defense against its tongue attack.

"Liz, Leafa, once we avoid the dive, we've got to use sword skills before it moves again. Try to aim for the underside of its body to flip it over."

"Okay." "Got it."

"Sinon, Yui," I continued, "follow up when the frog's stomach is exposed. Kuro, protect Yui."

"Roger that!" "Yes, Papa!" "*Grawr!*"

I felt sure that the two girls understood my point but wasn't as positive about the panther. Here was hoping, though.

The giant frog's suckered limbs made their way up the rock wall with ease. Another ten seconds until it reached the top again. Could we use the materials on hand to fashion a kind of trap where it was going to land? Like making a line of spiked logs—assuming such a thing existed in the Woodworking skill…

"Kirito!" Sinon shouted, startling me out of my thoughts. The Goliath Rana wasn't yet to the top of the dome, but its legs were bulging with tensed power.

"Kwah!"

I jumped backward desperately, right as the frog kicked off the wall. It obliterated the boulder before my eyes like a cannonball. Fist-sized chunks of rock struck my shoulder and leg. They dented my iron armor and caused notable HP loss.

Bastard!

I entered the stance for Rage Spike—a low thrusting skill—before I landed. You usually had to lean forward as far as possible right over the ground, so executing the proper motion while in the air was a very high-level technique.

My sword took on a pale-blue sheen as soon as my feet hit a shallow puddle. The instant the skill activated, I leaped forward, boosting the action. Water frothed to the sides as I charged at the throat of the briefly stunned frog.

Without missing a beat, Leafa came in from the right and Lisbeth from the left. They were using skills that targeted low, according to the plan. With this many attacks happening at once, there was no way we could fail to flip over the frog, no matter how big it was.

And in less than a second, my confidence turned to horror.

The Goliath Rana, which looked like a tiny mountain up close, suddenly flattened, as though all of its bones had vanished. It squashed itself absolutely horizontal against the ground, hiding its neck and belly. But I couldn't stop the sword skill. My sword hit the frog's snout, Leafa's katana and Lisbeth's mace hit its shoulders, and the dark-red skin dented inward.

It felt like slicing a huge blob of rubber. The tip of my sword sank into it, but I didn't feel like I was cutting *anything.* Then there was a huge resistance pushing back until it overpowered the thrust of the sword skill.

All at once, the three of us yelped as we were hurtled backward. There was no way to defend when your body was thrown into the air. The frog's mouth opened. Its vicious pink tongue withdrew, tensing, ready to spring forward like a fleshy spear.

Blaaaam!

A huge roar assaulted my eardrums. Sinon had fired her musket. The bullet split the frog's tongue, sending crimson damage effects spilling everywhere. It lost less than 10 percent of its HP, but the frog croaked and fell backward, exposing its soft-looking throat.

"Yaaaa!" "Raaaar!"

Yui executed the sword skill Vertical, and Kuro charged, its huge fangs exposed. Sword and teeth cut at the frog's throat from either side. There went another 10 percent of its HP.

Yui's and Kuro's simultaneous attacks might have done modest damage, but the real benefit was that they extended the toppling effects of our offensive. The frog landed on its back in the water, still exposed.

We have to add on! But Liz, Leafa, and I were still struggling from the knockback effect. The frog's short front legs and massive back legs flopped and flailed, as though it were going to leap upright again soon. Sinon was reloading and couldn't fire again yet.

This combination was largely a product of coincidence and probably couldn't be recreated a second time. If we missed out on the chance to extend this rally, our hopes of winning got smaller. I clenched my teeth, desperately trying to right myself. I reached out with my left hand, scratching at the empty air with my fingers, but my avatar cruelly continued to topple…

"Keeee!"

A high-pitched screech filled the air.

It wasn't the frog, and it couldn't have been any of us. Was it a fresh add—a new monster joining the fight? But what I saw leaping forward into the fray was not amphibian in nature. It was small, clad in simple clothes, and holding a rusty pitchfork in both hands—the trio of ratmen who had completely vanished from my mind.

They rushed to the flipped-over Goliath Rana and stabbed its pale belly deep with their pitchforks.

"*Errrbit!*" the frog roared furiously, jerking and contracting its entire body and bounding upright again like a spring-wound toy. The ratmen yelled "אא!" and retreated to the edge of the dome.

They didn't seem to be consistent participants in the battle, so having this brief bit of extra damage inflicted was a huge help. The HP bar of the frog was down 40 percent and had gone from white to a much yellower shade.

The Goliath Rana, now upright, leaped with a splash toward the wall, where it began to climb. Liz, Leafa, and I scrambled to our feet to prepare for one of its dive attacks.

After that sequence of events, it seemed clear that the Goliath Rana battle was one where it was difficult to hit its weak point, but once you did, there was a ton of damage to inflict. We could beat it after just two more times of flipping it over—maybe once, if we were lucky. But to do that, we needed to inflict damage on its mouth.

"Sinon, aim for the mouth!" I shouted. Sinon finished up reloading and said, "Got it."

To Lisbeth, I instructed, "When it dives for us, whack its head with your mace! It'll knock you back, but it'll give us a chance to attack its tongue…I think!"

"You *thiiink*?!" she howled but recovered quickly, squeezing the handle of her mace. "Fine, then! Let's do this!"

In tense fights that required great concentration, having a mood-maker like Lisbeth was a major help. That was a personal skill I could never replicate, I knew.

"Leafa, Yui, Kuro," I continued, "use your strongest sword skills when the frog flips over! Just watch out for its rear leg kick!"

"You got it!" "Yes, Papa!" *"Grar!"*

The three of them were ready. I glanced back toward the wall behind us for one final instruction.

"You folks, be ready to do that again, too!"

I was speaking to the trio of ratpeople. They did not respond. I had no choice but to trust they understood, because I had to focus on the top of the dome. The Goliath Rana was already 70 percent of the way up the wall. It could dive at us at any moment.

Next time, I'll dodge it right, I told myself, staring at the frog. Its limbs stopped moving. Those bulging eyes turned red.

But the next moment, something happened that I did not see coming.

Five or six warty bulges on the Goliath Rana's back protruded farther outward and shot deep-red flames. They diminished quickly but maintained their strength from that point on, flickering in place. I had no time to wonder what was going on before the frog opened its mouth and pointed at the floor of the dome.

It was over seventy-five feet away. The frog's tongue was long but not *that* long…

…Right?

What appeared in its gaping mouth was a glowing red circle. There were complex symbols inside the figure.

"A magic circle…?!" I gasped.

Leafa drowned me out, crying, "Look out, everybody!"

Before the words had left her mouth, an enormous ball of fire belched from the frog's mouth. I jumped to the right on sheer instinct, grabbed Yui, and dived into the nearby water.

There was a roar, and red filled my vision. Waves of heat broiled my back, lowering my HP bit by bit.

Once the explosion subsided, I stood up with Yui in my arms. "Is everyone all right?!"

Sinon, Lisbeth, and Leafa called back in the affirmative, and Kuro growled fiercely. The frog's fireball had evaporated one of the pools where it hit the floor, but nobody had been hit directly by the projectile. The ratpeople against the wall were fine, if clearly shaken by the event.

Up above, the Goliath Rana was still in the same spot, bulging and retracting its throat. It didn't seem likely to descend for the time being.

"A frog that shoots fire? It's like a slug with salt attacks...," I griped. Lisbeth retorted "You can't just make up sayings like they're...Actually, that *does* make sense." So my language skill retained its dignity, but the state of the battle was worse than before. The only long-range attack we had was Sinon's musket, so if the monster kept shooting fireballs from the ceiling, the fight would slip further out of our grasp.

It wasn't like we *had* to defeat this frog. As long as we escaped to the eastern side of the Giyoru Savanna with Sinon, we were fine. But that would mean climbing the sloped path around the wall up to the tunnel mouth, high up in the dome. The frog was unlikely to let us pass.

The sloped path...

"...Guys, I'm going to rush up the side of the wall and use a leaping skill to knock the frog down. You follow up the same way we said earlier!" I said, seizing on the idea I'd just had. My companions looked nervous, though.

"But then you're going to fall down with it, Big Brother. You might die if you fall from that height...," Leafa worried.

"I'll be fine," I reassured her. "I won't take any damage if I fall where the water's deep. This is the only way."

"..."

She closed her mouth, but the concern in her green eyes did not go away. Truth be told, I wasn't positive I *could* manage to fall into a spot of water deep enough to save me.

It was a desperate gamble, but as I lowered Yui to the ground to prepare, she abruptly announced, "No, Papa! I'll do that part!"

Shocked, I stammered, "N-no, you don't need to..."

"You have the highest attack of the party, so you should perform the follow-up on the vulnerable spot, not the first strike."

"But, Yui, you can't use Sonic Leap..."

"If I head back into the tunnel and get a running start, I can reach it with Vertical!"

"But..."

It seemed like the only thing I could do was offer rebuttals. Yui looked me in the eyes and said, "Papa, I don't want to spend my whole life being protected."

"..."

The earnest look in her eyes struck me as being very similar to Asuna's. And though I couldn't say for sure, I guessed it was probably similar to mine, as well.

"...All right. Go ahead," I told her and set her down.

A fair distance away, Sinon shouted, "It's moving again!"

I looked up at the dome and saw the giant frog plodding along horizontally. It was probably going to shoot another fireball. Perhaps it might aim at Yui as she was trying to climb the slope.

Lisbeth broke through my contemplation. "I'll pull its aggro! Just let her go!" She struck her round shield with her mace. Little ripple effects appeared from her shield, which meant she must have acquired some kind of taunting skill at some point.

The Goliath Rana stopped moving and began to pivot.

"Here I go!" Yui cried and took off running with her short sword in hand. Even I was stunned at the speed with which she leaped over rocks and puddles. She turned at the wall and sped up the path to the tunnel mouth.

The frog twisted its upper half backward and opened its mouth wide. The direction made it clear it was targeting Lisbeth.

"Get back, everybody!" she instructed.

I dutifully retreated, shouting, "Make sure you dodge it, Liz!"

"Trust in the quality of my shield!"

Does that mean what I think it does? I wondered, right at the moment that another red magic circle appeared in the Goliath Rana's mouth, shining brightly.

With an air-shaking roar, the beast shot a flaming projectile from its mouth. But Lisbeth stood her ground. She held the round shield up with her left arm and held her mace behind her.

The shield was made with the premium steel ingots she'd made from melting down Blárkveld. In keeping with the high Blacksmithing proficiency of its creator, the shield had to have a high defensive quality. But it couldn't possibly defend against a fire attack from a dungeon boss without damage.

My right foot tensed, ready to push me forward into action. But I grabbed my knee with my hand, holding it in place. If I jumped forward and got caught in the blast, I might not be ready to attack the frog after it fell. I had to trust in Liz and Yui and let them do what they were determined to do.

The eighteen-inch flaming ball struck the shield directly. It flashed, warping, billowing out red flames and black smoke that hid Liz from view. I shielded my face with my arms to protect against the explosion.

In the upper left, I saw Lisbeth's HP bar dropping. Down it went…70, 60, until it was below 50 in a blink…then stopped at around 40 percent.

"Liz!" I shouted, looking up.

Curled up in the center of the blast radius, Lisbeth lifted her thumb to reassure me. She could have darted out of the way and probably defended against it more successfully, but she took the hit to ensure it couldn't possibly be redirected toward Yui.

As for Yui, she was nearly to the top of the slope winding around the edge of the dome. Even I would have a hard time sprinting up the narrow ledge without a handhold of any kind. But Yui was pulling it off with aplomb—not because she was an AI but because we had raised her to have a real heart and real courage.

Once she reached the top of the path, she darted into the tunnel to give herself some running space to make the leap toward the frog.

"*Rrrbit...*," the Goliath Rana croaked, turning around so it could face the tunnel. That was bad...If it attacked with its tongue, it might knock Yui out of the air when she jumped.

"This way!" shouted Sinon. She pointed her loaded musket at the frog stuck to the ceiling of the dome and promptly pulled the trigger. The striker sent up sparks, and a moment later, the gun bellowed.

The bullet struck the Goliath Rana directly in the eye.

"*Gribbaaaw!*" the frog shrieked, turning once again.

Then a figure in white burst out of the tunnel.

She had a short sword readied at her right shoulder, her long black hair streaming behind her. The weapon was glowing blue, but the light was flickering. Executing a sword skill in midair when your stance wasn't solid was going to be very difficult for Yui, who hadn't practiced doing that, but she was managing to keep the effect glowing so far.

"Yaaaa!"

Her fierce war cry reached us down at the bottom. Once her right foot was out into the air, Yui activated Vertical. The game system boosted her small body, shooting her forward and leaving a brilliant slice in the air. The tip of the sword homed in on the frog's side. While it did not cut through the skin, the shock of the attack pulled the suckers from the frog's toes off the wall.

The frog's rubbery, resilient skin bounced Yui backward. The frog then followed her, falling off the ceiling and waving its limbs wildly in the air.

If she landed in the water, all was fine. But if she hit a rock, she would die. If I rushed to catch her, I wouldn't be there to attack the frog in time.

It was the biggest dilemma since the battle started. But then I heard an unfamiliar—but strangely familiar—voice.

"I got Yuippe!"

Thanks, whoever you are! I thought and made the motion for Sharp Nail, a three-part attack that was the strongest I could execute right now. Beside me, Leafa readied the same move, and Lisbeth recovered from the force of the fireball with her mace in hand. Sinon was holding a small laser gun rather than the musket, and Kuro bared its sharp fangs.

The Goliath Rana fell, belly up, onto one of the rock pillars and bounced high. When it landed a second time, I shouted, "Now!"

Leafa, Lisbeth, Kuro, and I struck the defenseless frog's stomach from all sides with swords, mace, and teeth. Its HP bar instantly took a huge drop, going under 20 percent. The four of us pulled back, and the ratpeople shrieked as they charged in, stabbing it with their pitchforks.

Ten percent left.

I struggled against the sword skill's delay, trying to give it just a normal swing to beat the frog for good. But a moment before I could, the frog opened its mouth, still on its back.

"*Grrrrrrg-gooooooo!*" it roared with fury, forming another big magic circle. If it spit a fireball this close, there was no way to dodge…

"I don't think so!"

Sinon leaped forward with great courage, jabbed her laser gun directly through the magic circle, and pulled the trigger.

It made a volley of sci-fi *pew-pew-pew-pew!* sounds, shooting light-green energy bolts into the Goliath Rana's open mouth and whittling down its HP bar. The magic circle around Sinon's arm flashed. Flames flickered in the frog's mouth, swirling into a tornado, rather than a fireball…

And then its HP was gone.

"*Gre-gurk*!" the frog croaked, and the crimson magic circle turned into black smoke that floated away. It looked very similar to the effect of a magic spell being fumbled in *ALO*.

The beast's massive body twitched a few times, getting steadily weaker...until it stopped moving altogether.

In *SAO* and *ALO*, a dead monster would promptly burst into blue particles, but here, the bodies stayed put—meaning you couldn't be *sure* it was dead yet. I was worried about Yui, but more important was making sure the frog had croaked its last. I took a step forward, sword at the ready.

Then something strange happened.

From the middle of the still, flipped-over frog, around the position of its heart, a red light appeared, rising silently in the darkness. We'd defeated many monsters by now, including the thornspike cave bear that was just as strong, but I hadn't seen this happen with any of them.

"Kirito, look...!"

Urged on by Sinon's voice, I took two steps, then jumped as high as I could, reaching for the red light. But the instant my fingertips grazed it, the light popped and vanished, just like a bubble. As I landed, I checked my hand, but there was nothing on my palm.

Suddenly, all of the party members were surrounded by blue rings of light. For an instant I panicked, thinking it was some kind of trap, but soon realized it was just the level-up effect. The frog was good and dead. A message appeared telling me I was now level-16, but I hastily got it out of the way and looked up.

Even in the darkness, Yui's white dress was easily noticeable. She hung in the air just below the tunnel exit, her skinny left arm clutched by the extended arm of someone else hanging upside down. That player had a rope tied around their ankle, which a different player was holding tight from the tunnel entrance.

Yui and the mysterious player were swaying on the rope, drifting left and right, while a faint creaking sound made it clear that the rope was not strong enough to hold the weight of two people and was steadily fraying.

The large man standing in the cave entrance steadily pulled the rope upward. I darted forward to the position beneath Yui and called up, "Hey, easy, easy!"

The man pulling the rope bellowed down, "I don't have enough rope to lower them down there, and the durability's going to wear out in less than twenty seconds!"

The other player—the man holding up Yui by the hand—replied, "Don't let that happen to me, Boss! Not after comin' as far as we did! You gotta pull me up!"

Strange, I thought, feeling a sense of déjà vu. *I could swear I've heard both of those voices before.*

I dug in my heels to stop. Waiting below them wouldn't help if I couldn't actually catch both Yui and the man together. I needed a cushion instead. If I set out all the hyena pelts in my inventory, that probably wouldn't be enough to absorb the damage from a fall that high.

There was only one thing that could work here. I turned around, raced back, and shouted to the others, "Help me carry this over, guys!"

Then I grabbed the leg of the dead Goliath Rana. Instantly, everyone else understood my meaning. Sinon jumped ahead of me, and Lisbeth and Leafa grabbed the left leg. The four of us began to drag the huge corpse.

With a quick yowl, Kuro bit the frog's side to help us push, and even the three ratpeople set down their pitchforks and assisted with the head. Once we got going, the body slid faster than I thought it would over the rocky ground. I checked over my shoulder as we pulled and saw that Yui was halfway up the thirty feet or so to the tunnel mouth, but the rope was visibly wearing out.

We were almost to the spot beneath the two of them when there was a heartless *snap!*

"Sorry, Kirito! Do something!" shouted the large man who'd been pulling the rope. I didn't have time to wonder how he knew my name.

"Aaaieeee!" wailed the other man. But it was admirable the way that he managed to pull Yui close to him and make sure she'd land on top of him, rather than the other way around. We had to make that gesture pay off.

"Yaaaa!" I bellowed, wringing out the last of my strength. A new message appeared, reading *Physique skill proficiency has risen to 4*, and the frog's body rose a tiny bit into the air. It landed in a puddle and stopped.

A second later, Yui and the man disappeared into the Goliath Rana's stomach. Even dead, the body retained its resilience, and they bounced back over three feet up into the air before landing again safely.

"Papa!" cried Yui, who hadn't made a sound while she was hanging or falling. She jumped onto me with arms spread wide. I grabbed her and hugged her little body tight, careful not to crush her against the metal armor.

"You did great," I whispered. "The way you pulled off Vertical in midair was masterful."

For the first time since the battle against the Goliath Rana started, Yui's voice trembled. "Yes…I tried really hard!"

Yui had never been in a battle herself. Having her first experience be against a terrible boss had to be overwhelming and terrifying in a way I couldn't imagine. And it wasn't some carefully modeled imitation of human emotion in typical AI fashion. At this point, Yui had surpassed the limits of top-down artificial intelligence and gained true emotions—in my opinion. It was the only explanation for her self-sacrifice, I thought, stroking her hair.

Just then, the man resting with his limbs splayed out on the frog's stomach sat up, grumbling, "Ninety-nine times out of a hundred, I'd have died right there…"

His short brown hair was pushed upward by a dark-red bandana. His face was long and thin, and scraggly hair dotted his chin. His armor was leather, and a curved blade rested on his left side.

When I first heard that voice, there were two arguing opinions in the back of my mind: *Could be* and *No way.* It seemed that the winner was, indeed, *Could be.*

"Klein…what are you doing here?" I wondered in awe.

The katana warrior (now a scimitar warrior?) I'd known since the *SAO* days spread his hands and complained, "Whoa, whoa, is that gonna be the first thing out of your mouth, Kiri, my man? We rushed over here thinkin' you were in trouble and needed help!"

"Yeah, and we appreciate it," Lisbeth interjected. "But how did you know we were here? Nobody contacted you on the other side, did they?"

"I'll answer that one," said another voice from above, causing us all to look upward.

Carefully descending the path around the side of the dome was an imposing-looking man, big and bald and barrel-chested. This was another familiar face, the ax warrior and merchant Agil. But on his back wasn't the trademark two-handed ax but a double-edged ax that was noticeably smaller—though still much bigger than *my* sword. Like Klein, he wore leather armor.

"Hiya, Agil," I said, bumping knuckles with him as he reached the floor. Then I greeted Klein the same way and asked, "So… how did you get here? Did you start in the ruins to the south like the other *ALO* players?"

"Yeah. And me and Klein were a day late. We finally got a chance to dive in tonight, and the grace period was long over, plus the map all around us had been picked clean. Somehow, I managed to meet up with Klein, and we figured we'd head for your log cabin…"

"Huh? How did you know where it was?"

"Asuna drew us a map by hand."

"Oh, really..." For a brief moment, I stopped to consider my girlfriend, the former vice commander of the Knights of the Blood, and her penchant for detail.

"Kiri, fess up. You completely forgot about us, didn't you?" Klein grunted reproachfully from the frog's stomach. He was absolutely right, but I wasn't going to let him know that.

"N-no...that's not true. I mean, you and Agil have to work on weekdays...so I was going to get in touch when things settled down..."

Agil crossed his arms and said, "Our place is closed today."

Klein followed up with, "And I took a half day and left after lunch."

"Dicey Café has irregular hours, and I can't read your mind to know when you'll take vacation days, Klein!" I argued.

Sinon stopped loading her musket to clear her throat. She grumbled, "Can you get on with it? We've got things to do."

"Oh, sorry, sorry." Agil got back to the topic at hand. "Anyway, we scraped together some gear and left the ruins for the forest, then got attacked by a trio of PKers. We had stone weapons, and they had iron, plus more armor, so I thought we were in big trouble."

"That's when you shoulda seen our combination work," Klein continued. "We chopped those PKers to pieces, one after the—"

Agil's deep voice cut him off. "You just hid behind me the entire time."

"Well, what was I supposed to do? My carryover skill was..."

Klein stopped himself there rather suspiciously. I assumed it was probably something about how his maxed-out Katana skill didn't apply to the scimitar he had equipped right now.

"So you took out the PKers?" I asked, looking to Agil.

"Yeah...they were an impromptu group, it seemed like, and their teamwork was horrid. So we managed to get through it. But I forgot we were after a grace period, and without thinking, I used an area-attack skill that took out all three of them," he said, scowling. Agil was a gentle giant of a player, and if the PKers had tried to run, he would have let them.

Leafa approached and patted his burly arm. "Don't let it bother you, Agil. If they were PKing, they must have known they were likely to get killed by one of their targets. We were attacked by a gang of them yesterday, and Kirito absolutely destroyed them all!"

"H-hey, it's not like I did it all on my own," I clarified hastily, then gestured to Agil. "And then what?"

He grinned and patted his gleaming leather armor. "The PKers helpfully dropped some leather armor as well as an iron ax and a scimitar. With that upgrade and the help of the map, we made it to the log cabin, where Asuna said she was worried about you guys and asked us to go help you."

"Oh, I see," I said, thanking my partner for her keen thinking. "But wait...How would she know which route we took? How did you two get to this cave...?"

Agil grinned once again, then jutted his chin toward Klein. The scimitar warrior scratched the bandana around his forehead, then inhaled, preparing himself to speak.

"That was through the use of the skill I brought over..."

"Huh? Your skill is Katana, right? What would that have to do with this?" Lisbeth said, speaking for my thought process, too. Leafa, Sinon, and Yui probably wondered the same thing. Everyone looked at Klein, who wore an expression that was impossible to classify.

"It ain't Katana."

"Huh?"

"I inherited Pursuit."

"*Huh?!*" we shouted together.

In *ALO*, the Pursuit skill was a useful one, highlighting the footprints of players and monsters and making it easier to find the materials you wanted, but it took great patience to power up, and very few players specifically worked at it. But Klein had worked his main weapon skill of Katana up to the maximum proficiency of 1,000, if I remembered correctly. If he didn't carry over Katana, then he must have also maxed out Pursuit…

"Why would you be so advanced in a skill like that?" Lisbeth asked, exasperated. Then she realized something and cried, "Oh! Unless you were using it to track and follow cute girls! You creep!"

"N-no! It's not that! I just worked at it in order to complete the chase quest that Skuld gave to me…"

"……Huh?" everyone but Agil muttered.

Skuld was the name of an NPC we met in the realm of Jotunheim, underneath Alfheim. She was a graceful beauty reminiscent of depictions of Norse Valkyries. Thinking back on it, I recalled that she had given Klein something when we parted ways. So it was an item that started a new quest…and that was the impetus for Klein to work the Pursuit skill up to the max?

"So…did you beat the quest?" I asked.

Klein shook his head sadly. "I was almost finished with it…and then *this* happened. I hope Skuld's all right…"

I decided not to ask him what would have happened if he'd managed to finish his Pursuit quest. Better to get back to the matter at hand.

"So you managed to catch up to us thanks to the Pursuit skill you carried over. But the proficiency would have gone down to 100, right? I'm amazed you were able to track us this far."

"Yeah, well…you can't actually choose to track a specific player's footprints at 100, but there was just one party's worth of prints on the plains. So I figured it must be you guys and followed them here."

"Ah, I see," I murmured, satisfied at last. I bowed to Agil and Klein. "You really saved our bacon. If you hadn't caught her, Yui would have fallen to the ground with the frog."

"Agil, Klein, thank you!" Yui added, bowing. Both of the big, burly men smiled with embarrassment.

"If only we could have made it in time for the battle," Agil said.

"I dunno. I'm not a fan of those slimy monsters," Klein muttered in a tone of voice that suggested he was not at all joking. I pointed at the object he was using as a seat cushion.

"You know that's the frog's carcass, right?"

"Huh…? Ueowaaaah!!" he shrieked, bouncing vertically into the air with his legs still crossed. Even Sinon laughed at that.

9

The three ratpeople fighting alongside Sinon were a minority people in the world of *Unital Ring* called the Patter. There were only a hundred or so of them living within the caves of this natural border wall.

Sinon encountered them within the cave and learned about the history of the Patter from an elder who could speak human language (i.e., Japanese). According to him, the Patter once lived in a great city on the northern side of the Giyoru Savanna, but a terrible natural disaster laid it to waste overnight, and the survivors were chased by the enormous carnivorous dinosaurs that prowled the plains and had to live in the caves within the wall instead.

The Patter had a legend that, far to the east beyond the wall, there was a rich, deep forest. Some of the younger members wished to travel there and live in the forest, but to get to the eastern side of the wall, they needed to pass through the dome where the ferocious giant frog lurked. A number of valiant warriors had tested the frog, and all had been killed, so the elder Patter had given up on the dream of crossing the wall. But Sinon needed to get through to the eastern side to meet up with us anyway, so three of the braver—by their standards, at least—young Patter joined her in an attempt to beat the frog.

The Goliath Rana, it turned out, was much tougher than she'd expected, based on the story, and her musket was less useful than she'd hoped. So despite her courage, Sinon considered retreat. That was when our group jumped in to help beat the frog, with great effort.

Regardless of the trouble, we had completed the biggest goal of the night, meeting up with Sinon, and had the added bonus of finding Klein and Agil, too. The only thing left to do should have been going back the way we'd come, but there was one more, rather unexpected, part of the story. We had extra members of our retinue—not just the three Patter who fought the Goliath Rana with us but an entire *twenty* of them.

"...Do you think this is some kind of quest, Kirito?" Lisbeth whispered to me. We were walking at the head of what was less a party and more a full-blown procession.

I thought it over and shook my head. "No...I don't think so... For one thing, I checked the quest tab of my menu earlier, and there was nothing written there..."

"When we reach the forest, do you think they're just going to peace out?"

"...Yerm."

"And do you think we're all going to reach the forest safely in the first place?"

"...Yerm."

"Is 'yerm' supposed to be a yes or a no?"

"Both."

She loudly and transparently exhaled, then looked over her other shoulder. "Leafa, is there something wrong with your brother?"

"Ha-ha-ha...Big Brother has a tendency to regress to his childhood now and then..."

That was a mean thing to say, but I didn't want to spend any time arguing. Ever since the twenty Patter expressed a desire to come with us, I'd been desperately thinking of a way to make everything work out.

I hadn't given Liz a positive or negative answer to her question about the Patter, but in truth, I couldn't imagine them surviving once we reached the log cabin's forest—which they called the Great Zelletelio Forest. There was plenty of water and food, yes, but also many monsters, and if they came across one of those thornspike cave bears, which were even stronger than the Goliath Rana, it would wipe out all twenty of them.

I didn't yet know what happened when the NPCs of this world died. Perhaps they would come back to life after a certain amount of time passed. But that didn't mean we could just abandon them to a cruel fate. We couldn't have beaten the frog or been reunited with Sinon without the three brave ratmen and their pitchforks.

On the other hand, it was going to be difficult to take in twenty Patter at the log cabin. They might all fit inside, but there were more of us now, too, which meant it was going to be nearly impossible to find enough floor space for everyone to lie down at night. I glanced over my shoulder, wondering what to do, and caught sight of Yui walking with Sinon.

She must have been overjoyed at the reunion, because she was holding Sinon's hand and talking excitedly. Although it couldn't have been true, it also seemed like she was just a bit taller than before. That had to be a trick of the mind after witnessing her growth as a warrior today. She claimed she wanted to be a mage, but I felt like she'd have been better off with Brawn or Swiftness, rather than Sagacity. For one thing, a day and a half had passed, and we still didn't even know how to learn the magic skills.

Just then, I had a sudden thought and hurriedly brought up my ring menu. Over on the inventory tab, I sorted my items, newest first, and saw an unfamiliar name at the top of the list.

Fire magicrystal.

Now that was an enticing name. I tapped it to bring up the item properties. Beneath the name and durability level was a short description: *A crystal made of the condensed essence of fire magic. Grants the fire magic skill. If already acquired, adds a small proficiency bonus.*

Let's gooo! I wanted to scream, but I held it in, lest I startle the nervous Patter. They were already afraid of Kuro, who was walking ahead of me.

It was clear to me now when I'd picked up the fire magicrystal. It was the red light that rose from the Goliath Rana's body. The moment I'd grabbed it, the item had gone directly into my inventory.

So why did the light appear from the Goliath Rana's body and not the thornspike cave bear's? Because the frog used fire magic. In other words, learning magic skills in this world required defeating a monster that used that kind of magic. It just wasn't clear if that could be any random monster or if it had to be a tougher, boss-type enemy.

I tapped the open properties window, and it created a smaller window labeled TIPS.

To use this item, you must materialize it, then crush it between your teeth.

"......"

That was an intense method, I had to say, but seeing that it had come from a monster's body, I supposed it made sense. I closed that notice, then hit the button on the properties window to make it appear in physical space.

The magicrystal was not a bodiless light, the way it appeared when I caught it. Now it was a translucent crystal less than an inch in size. It was a brilliant crimson color, with a tiny flame trapped in its center. All I had to do was crunch it between my teeth like a hard candy to earn the fire magic skill, but of course I wasn't going to do that. Instead, I turned and offered it to Yui.

"Here you go, Yui."

"...? What is it?" she asked, tilting her head. She got a good look at the magicrystal and beamed. "Ooh, it's beautiful, Papa! I'll take very good care of it!"

"No, don't do that...Try eating it."

"........What?"

It wasn't just Yui. Sinon, Lisbeth, and Leafa all looked skeptical.

I probably should have explained it from the start, but I was possessed by a desire to make the magic skill a fun surprise for her.

"You'll understand if you eat it. Give it a crunch?"

"......"

She gave me the exact same look Asuna did when she was feeling suspicious of me, but she popped the magicrystal into her mouth anyway. She rolled it around in her cheeks, then mumbled, "Papa, it doesm't tase like anyhing."

"Kirito, do you know what you're doing?" Sinon demanded. I reassured her that it was fine and that I had it under control.

"Don't suck on it, Yui. You have to bite through it."

"Oh...okay."

Yui took on a determined look, trapped the magicrystal between the molars on her right side, then closed her eyes and chomped down hard. It didn't make the crunching sound I expected but a high-pitched, ringing *craaaack*.

Flames burst out of Yui's mouth.

"Hwaaaaah!" Yui shrieked. I was about half as startled as she was, but there had been no HP loss. Lisbeth screamed "Fire, fire, fire!" and reached for her water to feed to the little girl, but the flames had already gone out.

"Hey, Big Brother! That was a really mean prank!" Leafa rounded on me, fists raised. I shook my head.

"N-no, no, it wasn't a prank! Did you get the message, Yui?!"

"Hwaaah...Oh, I did...It says, fire magic skill gain— What?!"

Yui's eyes flashed, and she instantly popped open the ring menu to check her skills tab. She tapped the top of the list of acquired skills and read the window that appeared.

"Wow, it says I can cast a magic spell called Flame Arrow!" she exclaimed to the shock of the others.

I beamed at my daughter and egged her on. "Well? Give it a go."

"Okay! It seems that magic in this world is executed with gestures, unlike in *ALO*. Let's see..." She looked up from the window and arranged her hands in front of her body. "This is the basic gesture for fire magic, it says."

She clenched her left hand into a fist, then extended the fingers of her right hand in a row and struck them against the fist from a diagonal angle. A red aura bloomed around both hands.

"The next gesture will indicate the magic spell to use."

She opened her left hand and thrust it forward, then raised her right hand above her shoulder, like pulling back a bow. A glowing red line appeared in the air, connecting the two hands. She looked around quickly, then pointed her left hand at a rock about sixty feet ahead of us.

"This will be the activation gesture. Apparently, the more accurate the physical gesture and rhythm, the more powerful and precise the magic will be."

She clenched both hands tightly. A small magic circle appeared before her left hand, and the red line turned into a flaming arrow that shot forward with a *fwoosh!* It arced very slightly and struck the rock true, causing a small explosion. We all murmured with appreciation and applauded. I expected the Patter to be alarmed, but they were not *that* timid. Instead, they began to squeak among themselves.

The spell couldn't compare to the high-level magic used by master mages in *ALO*, but it was the first magic I'd seen here, aside from the Goliath Rana's fireballs, and I felt greatly emboldened by it. And you could increase magic skills not just by using them but also by consuming more magicrystals, so there were more avenues to improving them than there were with the weapon skills. Hopefully, I'd get a chance to learn magic eventually, but for now it was better to support Yui's growth.

"How much of your MP did that cost, Yui?"

"Um, my maximum MP is 157, and that cost 15, so it was a little less than ten percent."

"Mm-hmm…And what's the speed of your natural regeneration?"

"With my Concentration ability at a rank of 1, it takes six-point-two seconds to recover a single magic point. That means it takes ninety-three seconds to recover the cost of a single Flame Arrow.

It's not suited to rapid, consecutive use, I'd say," she admitted, looking downcast.

I rubbed her head. "Don't worry about it, kiddo. That's what the natural regeneration is in most games. I'm sure we'll get some MP potions soon or learn how to make them from ingredients."

"I hope so..."

"I'll make sure to handle all of that—you don't need to worry about it, Yui. For now, I'd say you should use that spell whenever your MP fully recovers. That way you'll gain proficiency gradually over time."

"Okay! I'll do my best!" she said, smiling at last.

Leafa exclaimed, "In that case, I wanna learn the wind magic skill soon! If you find a wind magic stone, Kirito, give it to me!"

"Sure thing. I wonder what'll come out of your mouth if you eat the wind stone," I said purely out of curiosity. But for some reason, Leafa pounded me under the left arm where I had no armor. I made a big show of grunting in pain.

In the back of the party with Agil, Klein complained loudly enough that everyone could hear him,

"Awww, man. Is it gonna be like this in *UR*, too?"

The travel back east over the Giyoru Savanna was stunningly easy compared to what we went through to get to Sinon. Knowing where to go and having the anticipation of home sweet home waiting at the end made it possible to actually enjoy the scenery on the way.

As usual, hyenas and bats interrupted our travel, but we were massively more powerful now, and there were no more terrifying hailstorms along the way. Even water and food, the most troublesome aspects of all, turned out fine, thanks to the huge stockpile of frog meat from the Goliath Rana's body, plus the natural spring water from the cave. The girls did not seem to enjoy seared frog meat, however.

What was very lucky was that in addition to the water and food, the cave contained a bunch of iron and copper ore. This went to the women, who resisted packing frog meat into their inventories and the little packs the Patter wore. Once we were able to smelt the ores at our base, we'd have our ingot needs met for quite a while.

We finally finished crossing the Giyoru Savanna again after ten thirty and entered the Zelletelio Forest. We just had to walk through the woods for a bit, cross the river, and we'd be back at our log cabin.

The moment the huge trees came into view ahead, the twenty Patter leaped about and hugged one another with excitement. Some even burst into tears. To them, the Zelletelio Forest was a promised land spoken of for generations, so it made sense that they'd be ecstatic, but the forest was not safe, and certainly no paradise.

Since Sinon was the one person who could speak any Patter, I asked her to tell them not to let their guards down before we went inside. We continued east, defeating the new types of monsters inside, until eventually the light began to flicker in the distance.

"Oh! That's the river! We're almost home!" Leafa cheered and began to rush ahead.

"Don't run in there! There are monsters in the river," I shouted, starting to give chase along with Kuro—until Leafa came to an abrupt stop. "Hey, what's the…?"

"Big Brother, look!!" she exclaimed, pointing. When I followed her finger, my heart nearly stopped beating.

Beyond the trees lining the far bank of the river, the night sky was burning red. I pulled up my map to check our location. In the direction we were facing was…the log cabin. I listened closely, and behind the roar of flames, there was the faint sound of metal clashing. When it caught the burning odor on the night breeze, Kuro growled softly.

"Asuna…Silica…Alice!"

I began to run toward the cabin, thinking of the three we'd left watching over it. The others hurried quickly behind me. I crossed the rocky riverside, looking for a spot where the water was shallow, and made it over the river there. Among the trees on the eastern side of the river was a huge divot where a piece of New Aincrad fell. The cabin would be shortly past that.

At this point, I could clearly see the flames through the trees. The clashing of metal on metal was no longer muffled. It seemed undeniable that the cabin was under attack, probably by a group of PKers like Mocri and his gang last night.

I wanted to rush to aid those I'd left behind, but the first order of business was deciding what to do about the twenty Patter. Their armor was of simple cloth make, and their weapons—pitchforks and scythes—were basically converted tools. Based on the fight with the Goliath Rana, I estimated they were only level-2 or level-3. If they rushed into a battle full of sword skills, some of them were going to die.

"Sinon, tell the Patter to hide and wait here!"

She passed my message on, but after just two seconds of discussion, they all shook their heads. It was difficult to register finer emotions in their big black eyes, but I could sense the outrage in their voices as they squeaked "אאא!"

"She says they want to fight, too."

I almost replied with "She?" but decided the details could wait until later. It didn't solve my worry, but we didn't have time to talk this over.

"Fine, just tell them to stick together. Don't split up."

While Sinon translated that for the ratpeople, I turned to Leafa, Lisbeth, Klein, Agil, and Yui.

"We don't know who's attacking or how many of them are there, but if we take too long observing, it'll leave the three of them in danger. We'll have to charge in, take the enemy by surprise, and then adjust on the fly."

"If you want to fight with improvisation, I'm your man!" Klein boasted, thumping his leather armor. I was kind enough not to remind him that his best skill right now was merely Pursuit.

With our strategy set, we started running.

The furrow in the earth heading to the northeast from the river was our path to the cabin. It didn't take long for red flames to come into view. Fortunately, it wasn't the cabin itself that was burning but the ancient spiral pines growing around the clearing. The ten-foot stone wall and wooden gate were still standing strong.

Atop the wall, there were irregular flashes of silver light. That was combat in progress. Our friends and the invaders were battling atop that foot-wide wall. By the light of the burning trees, I could see what looked like ten—no, more than twenty—figures launching themselves at the wall and attempting to climb it. Perhaps they'd lit the spiral pines for more light.

A particularly loud *clang!* sounded, and one of the attackers atop the wall tumbled to the ground. Asuna, her long brown hair flying, quickly turned the other way and thrust her rapier at another invader climbing the wall. Not far away, Alice and Silica were fighting just as hard. It seemed the three of them were focusing primarily on knocking the attackers back off the wall.

Their intentions were clear. They were buying time, trusting that we'd return with Sinon to help, and doing whatever they possibly could to protect our home until then.

Based on how burnt the spiral pines were, the battle must have started over thirty minutes ago. The invaders could wait and rest on the ground, but Asuna, Alice, and Silica had to keep fighting on that narrow catwalk. Their HP and willpower had to be close to the breaking point, I assumed. Another enemy approached Asuna from behind. Silica and Alice were too busy fighting to notice. The flames in the trees were roaring all around, so I knew they wouldn't hear if I yelled from a distance.

Even still, I sucked air into my virtual lungs, desperate to warn Asuna.

But before I could let it out, there was a gunshot behind me.

The enemy who was sneaking up behind Asuna reeled backward, took a few toppling steps, then fell on the inside of the wall. Sinon had picked him off with the musket. Her aim was as precise as ever, but if he was on the inside, he'd be able to open the bolt on the gate.

But my concerns were wiped away by a ferocious "*Quaaack!*" from what could only be Aga. Asuna's pet long-billed giant agamid was taking care of anyone who fell on the inside of the stone wall.

The sound of the musket firing was thankfully not too loud for the burning spiral pines to cover up. I gestured to Sinon to reload, then picked up my running speed.

Just ten yards separated me from the enemy group.

"Kuro, protect Yui!"

"*Gaurr!*" the panther snarled. I held my sword above shoulder level.

In yesterday's battle, I'd had to fight PKers in my underwear with a stone knife, which had been quite a struggle—it wouldn't go like that today. My sword vibrated subtly, taking on a light-green hue. The instant I sensed the skill's activation, I hurtled myself off the ground: Sonic Leap.

At last, one of the attackers noticed me.

"Hey, behin—"

But a tenth of a second later, my sword sank deep into his left shoulder. Red HP bars appeared over all their heads at once, a sign they had formed a raid party together.

The armor of the man was leather, and he carried an iron ax. I couldn't tell if that was what he'd brought from *ALO* or if he'd acquired both here, but like I had with Mocri's group last night, I didn't think it was low-level gear.

Still, thanks to rank-5 Brawn and rank-1 Bonebreaker, my single skill took over 80 percent of his HP. It slammed him to the ground and bounced him back upward, where an orange line split his left pec from behind. That was not a snipe shot from Sinon but Yui's Flame Arrow. It eliminated the little HP he had remaining, and he fell to the ground again. The ring-shaped cursor spun and grew, showing numbers where the HP bar had previously been: *0001:01:41:26.*

One day, one hour, forty-one minutes, and twenty-six seconds. That was how long this man had survived in *Unital Ring.*

The rotating numbers then disappeared, and the spindle-shaped axle of the cursor shot downward, piercing the man's body. The soulless avatar, equipment and all, morphed into a plethora of rings that quickly unfolded into tiny ribbons that rose into the sky.

Right on cue, cries arose.

"Enemy attack! Enemy attaaack!"

"They came up from behind! Trap them and crush them!"

These came from a nearby player with a shield and a spearman who seemed to be the leader of the group.

I found it highly offensive that *they* were calling this an "enemy attack," but now wasn't the time to quibble with terminology. Invaders with swords and spears immediately charged toward me from either side along the curved stone wall. About half of them had iron weapons, and the remainder had stone. If they were able to produce iron, they would have outfitted all of them with iron weapons before invading, so I assumed that, like with Mocri's group, either their inherited gear didn't hit the Equip Weight limit or they'd bought, found, or stolen their weapons somewhere along the way.

In that case, where had they found out about the log cabin? It didn't look to me like they'd been exploring along the riverside and randomly spotted the crash marks. I couldn't be sure yet, but I got the impression that these people knew about the base here and prepared as much as they could before attacking. Had Mocri or his friends leaked our info in revenge? They didn't seem so vindictive that they'd do something that wouldn't earn them anything in return…

But within the compressed time-space of my mind, I heard Mocri's mocking voice in my ears again.

Well, that's just what Sensei teaches. Don't only look at one part of the opponent; grasp the whole. Then you'll know what they're aiming for—and what they don't like, you see.

It was what Mocri said when he had me on the ropes in our one-on-one fight. His Sensei—someone who taught them the ropes of PvP combat—was still alive in the world of *Unital Ring.* If this Sensei was pulling the strings behind this attack, too, then I had to assume these twenty-something combatants were all similarly well-versed in PvP tactics.

The only question now was whether this Sensei had taught them more than just one-on-one combat, like also how to fight as a group. Either way, I should assume they knew.

In less than a second, I'd arrived at the answer. I called out to my companions, "Into the woods! Don't let them team up on you!"

Agil immediately replied, "We can't! The fire's in the trees!"

"...!"

I sucked in a sharp breath, looked around, and saw that the flames burning the spiral pines had already spread to the undergrowth. If you jumped among those flames, you'd burn to a crisp in moments.

That was when I realized the attackers weren't burning the forest around the cabin for light but as a means of preventing guerrilla tactics against themselves. To back that conjecture up, the groups coming at us from the sides were led by shield-bearing tanks flanked by attackers with swords and axes, then debuffers with long weapons in the rear—an orthodox battle formation. The silver lining was that they had no mages, but that wasn't going to make things any easier for us.

Atop the stone wall, the girls were still fighting bravely. Asuna glanced back toward me for the briefest moment, and sparks flew when our eyes met.

She didn't seem to have any secret comeback plans up her sleeve, but it was clear she was bristling with the intent to protect our house, no matter the cost. The trio we'd left behind trusted in our return and had focused on knocking the invaders off thc wall. We had to make their efforts count.

Our advantages were Lisbeth's excellent iron weapons, Yui's fire magic, the twenty Patter, and Sinon's Hecate II. The only one of those things that had the potential to overturn the massive numerical disadvantage we were suffering was the Hecate, but Sinon said she had only six of its bullets left. It could defeat a dragon if the shot hit a vital point—she said she'd killed a giant dinosaur with it—but six shots wasn't going to be enough to defeat a group of over twenty players. This wasn't the right time to use up all of the greatest firepower in the entire world of *Unital Ring.*

"Hey, what are we gonna do, Kiri?!" exclaimed Klein nervously, holding his thin scimitar. "If we're just gonna go for it, I'm with ya!"

"It's too early to resort to desperation. There's got to be a way to turn this around."

"Yeah, but when they've got such a tight formation, there's no proper way to break them down."

Klein was right; the enemy was not rushing but carefully closing the distance, keeping their shield users front and center. If we panicked and used sword skills, the tanks would just guard, and they'd be able to pick us off with counterattacks. It was almost like they knew we were built for attacking, not so much for defense.

Should we retreat to the river? But then the attackers would just continue their siege of the log cabin. Feeling the pressure from the enemy, Kuro growled from the rear, where it was guarding Yui. Behind them, the Patter were huddled together, speaking nervously.

If I were an utterly ruthless leader, I'd order them to charge into the enemy's midst and cause chaos so we could pick off the tanks. But I couldn't do that, of course. They had defeated their nemesis, the Goliath Rana, and made their way to the promised land of the Great Zelletelio Forest at last. Yes, there were dangerous monsters in the area anyway, but the very last thing I wanted was for them to die because of a squabble between players…

"…Oh!" I gasped.

I wasn't sure if it was an advantage or not, but there *was* one major uncertain variable in this forest. And if we could bring that into the battle, the attackers would no longer be so confident.

"Klein, Agil," I murmured to the two at my sides. "Throw all the frog meat you have into the flames."

I opened the ring menu and got busy without waiting for an answer, materializing all of the Goliath Rana meat I had filling up my inventory capacity. Bright-red chunks of flesh appeared atop the window, and I grabbed them and tossed them into the blaze to the left.

Within a few moments, Klein and Agil began doing the same thing. It was only the fact that we'd known one another for so long that kept them from wondering why we were busying ourselves with such a ridiculous task, given the present danger. Although if this *didn't* work, they were bound to lose a lot of confidence in me anyway.

"...What are they doing? Clearing out their junk?" asked one of the enemy fighters.

Another player replied, "They're cooking meat. What, are they gonna lure us out with food?"

"They don't think we're NPCs, do they?"

As they bantered, the frog meat cooked in the flames, creating a fragrant smell. The pink was a little *too* bright, but the meat was quite a fine ingredient, and it somehow smelled like we'd added black pepper and rosemary, just from being seared in the fire.

That alone, of course, was not going to make the attackers give up. Their spearman leader called out from the back, "Let's finish them off before they try something funny. Go to plan B!"

The rest of the group called out, "Yes, sir!"

But there was no way to know what kind of strategy plan B was. There was a deep rumbling from the forest, like a gigantic mortar and pestle grinding.

"Grrrrr..."

There it was.

The ground began to tremble. A new kind of horror chilled my spine. The frog meat had brought that uncertain variable into play—and it was a double-edged sword.

The left of the two groups of enemies visibly began to panic.

"Hey, there's something behind us…"

"Gurrraaaa!"

The roar was like thunder, and one of the nearby burning spiral pines snapped at the base. A tremendous four-legged beast, over six feet tall even with all of its feet on the ground, emerged from the flames. That was the tyrant of the forest, the creature that had terrified us last night—the thornspike cave bear. The smell of the frying frog meat had stimulated its hunger; drool hung from its thick teeth, and its red eyes looked greedily upon the scene.

"Aaaah!"

An enemy fighter charged, thrusting out his sword. The bear was unimpressed and jumped with surprising speed, easily swiping the attacker out of the way.

"Gaaah!"

He slammed against the stone wall around the cabin with a nasty crunch, as light as if he were a scrap of cloth, and bounced back about ten feet before hitting the ground. The core of his cursor shot down and disintegrated his avatar, which turned into a tangle of ribbons that flew into the sky.

It wasn't the heaviest armor, but that player had fairly decent equipment, and he lasted all of a single swipe. The thornspike cave bear had even higher stats than I'd realized. It couldn't use magic, so its physical attack power was definitely higher than the Goliath Rana's.

This told me that it was indeed a true miracle that we'd beaten the bear last night by rolling those logs off the roof. Klein, Agil, and I slowly backed away from the creature.

I'd expected the players to panic and flee in various directions after they saw their companion slaughtered in a single second, but I was disappointed. The spearman recovered from the shock immediately, raised his weapon—a fancifully designed fauchard, a kind of hooked polearm that was clearly inherited from his previous game—and bellowed, "Don't panic! A and B teams, regroup and take boss formation!"

His hair was a dark-red color, and his skin was bronzed. In *ALO*, he would be a salamander. I didn't recognize him, but I could imagine he'd been one of the lancers serving under General Eugene in the territorial wars.

In that case, I couldn't help but wonder, who was this Sensei capable of enlisting such talented, hardcore players...?

The two groups of attackers quickly assembled, forming one massive raid party. The formation of tanks, attackers, and debuffers was the same as before. Even the three fighting with Asuna, Alice, and Silica jumped down to join the group.

"Grrraaaah!!"

The thornspike cave bear roared and scratched at the ground, then launched into a tremendous charge. It was the same thing it did when it nearly destroyed the wall of the cabin.

Claaank! A resounding crash filled the air. The four tanks formed a line and just barely managed to absorb the bear's momentum. I couldn't help but exclaim "Whoa," under my breath.

But now wasn't the time to sit around and be impressed. We had to make full use of this time while things were at their most chaotic.

"Kirito! What are we doing?!" Lisbeth demanded, yanking on my arm.

I thought hard. The enemy had their sides exposed to us, so I wanted to attack, but if we drew the bear's attention, that would be making a bad situation worse.

Though I didn't like it, perhaps it would be best to sit back and watch them fight for now. If the bear was winning, great, and if it lost, it was sure to inflict plenty of damage on the players, making it easier for us to finish them off...

It was a cruel but rational tactic. But I didn't get a chance to explain.

"Kirito," said a voice from the right. Somehow Silica was there, not on top of the stone wall anymore. I was going to applaud her long, tiring struggle to defend the cabin, but she held out her hand to stop me. "Kirito, that huge bear is the thornspike cave bear you wanted me to tame, right?"

"Er…yeah, that's right. But I was thinking more in the long term…"

"But even still, if I'm going to turn it into a pet one day, I can't just abandon it to a horrible fate now," she said, very determined. Pina, the little dragon perched atop her head, cried "*Kyuu…*"

Whether that bear wins or loses, the one you're going to try taming in the future is a different individual, I could have said, but I didn't. Silica had been a beast-tamer ever since *SAO*, and it wasn't that kind of logical decision on her part. If we used *this* thornspike cave bear as a sacrificial pawn now, then when she eventually tamed some other bear, she wasn't going to feel truly connected to it. I understood that mindset, and I respected it.

I stared back into those determined eyes, then looked at Asuna and Alice atop the distant wall. They stood there, rapier and longsword in hand, hair swaying in the wind, and nodded as though reassuring me that they'd accept my decision, whatever it was.

"…All right. We'll let the bear handle the front line and attack from the rear," I announced. Silica exclaimed "Okay!" and Klein smacked me on the back with a "That's the spirit!"

Up ahead, the thornspike cave bear and the invaders were locked in fierce combat. The bear's main attacks were swiping with its front paws and charging, and the four tanks were desperately defending against them so that the swordsmen could damage it from the sides, and the spearmen from the back row. Their teamwork was too practiced to be an impromptu raid party, but I hadn't made contact with the bear yet, so I couldn't see if they were doing any real damage to its HP bar. Depending on our timing, we might wind up battling against a furious thornspike cave bear at peak health, but if that happened, then so be it.

I made eye contact with the others to get us on the same page, then lifted my sword, waited for the bear to charge once again—and swung it down.

Agil, Klein, and I sprinted forward in a row. We were heading for the spearman leader, who was taking charge from the middle of the back row. Agil took the first attack by using the wide-range Two-Handed Ax skill Whirlwind, knocking away the two players guarding the leader.

"Whoa..."

"They're here!" shouted the two as they fell, drawing the attention of the entire back row of the enemy. Another two players rounded on Agil with admirable reflexes, taking advantage of his post-skill delay.

"I don't think so!"

Klein used the basic Reaver skill for one-handed curved swords, and I used Vertical. The perfectly synchronized attacks took down the two foes.

We'd sent four enemies into a tumbled state, but now all three of us were stuck in a delay. The enemy leader reared back with his fauchard and bellowed, "It was poor form to attack us now, Kirito!"

How do all of these people know who I am? I grumbled to myself as I watched the sharp tip of the fauchard glow aquamarine. That was the color of Whirlpool, an area skill for two-handed spears. It was less powerful than the Two-Handed Ax skill Whirlwind, but it caused a dazed Debuff effect.

At that point, I finally saw the name *Schulz* above the enemy leader's HP bar. I didn't recognize the name, but I had a feeling that, like Mocri, I wasn't going to forget it now.

Just before his Whirlpool could knock all three of us off our feet, there were two different bursting sounds behind it, and two different kinds of fire struck Schulz's chest and shoulder. That was Yui's magic and Sinon's gun. He lost his skill opportunity and faltered backward. Lisbeth and Silica jumped in, adding on with normal mace and dagger attacks and knocking him to the ground.

Released from my delay at last, I leaned forward as far as I could go and raised my sword.

If I hit him with all three blows of Sharp Nail, I could probably take Schulz's HP down to zero. But if I executed it the way it normally worked, the slashes wouldn't hit a target collapsed on the ground. At times like that, you had to sink down close to the ground—but take a stance that was too irregular, and the sword skill wouldn't work.

So I dug my toes into the ground in an effort to get more support, and I entered the proper motion as low as I possibly could. My iron sword glowed red, vibrating at a high pitch.

The instant I launched myself off the ground, I met Schulz's gaze.

His eyes contained surprise, frustration, and something else. Doubt…? About what?

Very belatedly, I realized I wanted to hear what he had to say. How did he learn where the log cabin was? How did he put together such a large force? Why did they attack like this? But it was too late. I couldn't stop the sword skill once it was in motion.

With the help of the game system, I leaped five yards in a single step. Schulz didn't bother to get up. He did hold up his fauchard in an attempt to guard, but he estimated my slash being too high. The first swing of Sharp Nail, coming in a ground-hugging dash, snuck past the handle of the polearm and hit Schulz in the neck.

My sword bounced back and struck again a second and third time, ignoring the laws of inertia. The motions carved red claw marks in the air that mingled with the bloodred damage effects.

His HP bar promptly emptied.

"Kirito…you're…really…"

Before he could finish, the spindle from his HP bar pierced his body and dissolved it into rings.

I'm really what?!

I didn't scream the question on my mind because it didn't seem like appropriate parting words for a man who was leaving this world forever after fair combat. Plus, the fighting wasn't done yet.

I straightened and looked at the enemy players around me. "Your leader is dead! We won't pursue if you run for your lives now!"

When fighting the pack of goblins in the cave near Rulid in the Underworld, that was enough to make the goblins split immediately, but the players in my vicinity only gave me suspicious looks.

"Shut up! We can't turn tail and run *now*!" shouted one of them. He charged with a short spear, which I hastily blocked. That attitude made sense, so I switched to battle mode, pushed back, and blew him off his feet with Vertical.

From that point on, it was an all-out melee, with no tactics or teamwork or planning, just chaos.

Half the enemy fighters were dealing with the thornspike cave bear, so I made sure not to get too close to them, and I focused on cutting down the other half of their group. Sinon's musket and Yui's fire magic were a huge help, and they identified each player who tried to unleash a major sword skill to counter me, and took them out. That let me focus on only the opponent I was facing at each moment. Of course, the enemy wasn't stupid, either, so some of them tried to neutralize Sinon and Yui, but Kuro and the group of Patter helped prevent that.

What really decided the course of battle was Asuna and Alice, who determined that no one was going after the cabin anymore and jumped down from the wall to join the fight. They took out their frustration over the long defensive battle against the enemy and, in less than five minutes, eliminated the eight members of the rear guard.

When we finally got a moment to breathe, I turned to the two of them and said, "Good job keeping things under control. Sorry we're so..."

"Groaaagh!!"

A roar at a higher volume and ferocity than before cut me off. I looked to my left and saw the eight remaining attackers and, beyond them, the thornspike cave bear with its front legs open wide. We'd seen that movement last night. And it meant the bear's next attack was…

"Uh-oh…Everyone, hit the deck!!" I shouted, throwing myself to the ground. Half a second later, my friends did the same.

The next moment, the lightning pattern in the bear's chest flashed.

A blizzard of needles sprayed outward, blasting the eight enemy combatants.

Even wearing her plate mail from the old game last night, Alice was brought half to death by the attack. But I wasn't able to see its effects on the players. I had to keep my face pressed to the ground because a stray quill grazed the top of my head.

I could hear the metallic needles striking the dirt, trees, and rocks all around us. Thankfully, I could still see the party's HP bars with my face in the dirt, so I prayed that no one would die before the attack was over.

Someone off to the side behind me shrieked "Yeow!" and Klein's HP bar took a big hit. Agil suffered some damage next, and then one quill pierced my left shoulder. If you couldn't even avoid the quills while flat on the ground, then the only ways to avoid them were to burrow underground or fly in the air. It seemed like a game-breaking design…but then again, a lot of this was our fault for being in a place over fifteen miles away from the starting point. I prayed to myself, *Okay, okay, we shouldn't be here. Just give us the chance to gain levels like we should!*

With one last jab in the dirt just inches from my nose, the storm of needles finally ceased.

I looked up carefully to see the thornspike cave bear lower its front legs to the ground and the eight players closer to us standing in a huddle. The four tanks were in a row, shields raised, with the four damage dealers hiding behind them. They had seemingly blocked the hail of spikes up close, an admirable bit of bold strategy and defensive power…

But then the sharp spindles in the middle of the ring cursors over their heads shot downward together. Eight avatars unraveled as one, sending millions of ribbons flying up into the night sky.

When the ribbons were gone, a group of black bags containing their belongings fell to the ground with a thud, but now was not the time to be distracted. From my stomach, I groaned, "No way…"

The thornspike cave bear grunted. Its shining red eyes glared at us. The bear was clearly targeting us, but I couldn't decide on a moment's notice if we should run or fight yet.

I'd taken one of the needles to my shoulder, so I could see the bear's cursor. It was at a bit above 60 percent health. The attackers had put up a good fight against the bear, but as I feared, it was still in quite good condition. With our group, I knew we had a better than zero chance of winning, but I couldn't be sure we'd triumph without fatalities.

No, wait a second. We weren't talking about fighting *the bear…*

That was when, emerging from the back and leaping past me, Klein, and Agil, a small figure made its appearance. It was Silica, Pina on her right shoulder and her hands empty. She approached the cave bear.

"H-hey, Silica!" I called out, getting up off my stomach.

She didn't turn back. "Let me handle this!" she hissed.

I understood, of course, that she wasn't talking about killing the bear but taming it. But that honestly seemed even harder than beating it. It was practically a miracle that I'd tamed Kuro the lapispine dark panther, but that happened when the both of us were taking shelter from the hailstorm, and it might have been a factor in my success.

On the other hand, the thornspike cave bear was in an enraged state after suffering many attacks over a long period, and even after slaughtering its eight attackers in an instant, it showed no signs of being satisfied. This was the reverse of the situation with Kuro, and it just didn't seem like a beast that Silica could conquer without inheriting her Beast-Taming skill.

But she approached the bear without fear, despite its bared fangs and menacing growl. In its paw, it was clutching a large blob of something. It was a piece of frog meat, well-done from the flames.

Instantly, I realized what I should be doing.

"Klein, Agil, go find the meat from the woods."

"G-got it."

"Sure thing."

We moved carefully, staying low and keeping Silica in our sights so as not to aggravate the bear. The fire had finished burning through all the spiral pines around the log cabin and was mostly out by now. We looked around the blackened ground, picking up hunks of sizzling frog meat and placing them back in our virtual item storage.

Silica, meanwhile, was within six feet of the growling thornspike cave bear, and she carefully tossed a chunk of meat. "Dinnertime, Mr. Bear," she said.

"*Grrgroaaah!*" it roared in response.

The thornspike cave bear stood up on its rear legs and brandished a menacing paw with knifelike claws. Upright, it was easily ten feet tall, and Silica was the smallest of our group after Yui. The difference in size couldn't have been starker, but physical size did not correspond to avatar strength in a VRMMO. Even still, I could practically see one vicious swipe of its paws disintegrating Silica the way it just did to those other players.

But that didn't happen.

Instead, the bear lowered its paws and returned to all fours. It snuffled at the frog meat in front of it, then took the chunk into its mouth, chewed a few times, and swallowed it.

"..."

I stopped collecting meat for a moment to watch the face-off between Silica and the bear. She was probably already seeing a circular beast-taming meter for her target. She waited for the right timing, then offered it more meat from her other hand. The bear took it right away.

When she opened her inventory, hands empty, I quickly hissed to Agil and Klein, "Trade me all the meat you've picked up."

It wasn't just Agil and Klein; I received trade windows from Leafa, Asuna, and Alice as well. I smacked the YES buttons in quick succession, then snuck within eight feet of Silica, the maximum distance for a trade request. She accepted my trade as soon as it went through, meaning Silica had all of the cooked frog meat in her inventory now.

The only thing left for us to do was pray.

Silica took cues from a meter that only she could see, tossing the pieces of frog meat one after the other. The bear bit and swallowed them in succession, with no sign of growing tired. There were over thirty pieces of meat I'd traded to Silica, but at the current rate, they were going to be gone within three minutes. If that wasn't enough to successfully tame the beast, we were back to the question of whether to fight or run.

Over her shoulder, I could see the inventory display of *Seared Goliath Rana Meat* dwindling. Ten pieces went down to five, then three, two, one…zero.

After tossing the final piece of meat, Silica whispered tensely, "The meter's been stuck at ninety-nine percent for a little while."

"…Okay, I'm sure there's one more piece of meat we missed. We'll go find it," I said, turning back to the forest.

But Silica shook her head. "No, another piece of the same meat isn't going to make up that one percent. I'm going to try taming it in this state."

There was already a long rope in her left hand. If she looped it around the thornspike cave bear's neck and tied it tight, the beast-taming attempt was successful, but I couldn't help but feel that the missing 1 percent was going to be the deciding factor.

"Wait, maybe there's some other food…"

I opened my inventory, scrolling through it in a hurry. I had a ton of random materials in there, considering that we'd only been in this virtual world for a day and a half, but almost no food ingredients. Hyena meat, salamander tail, bat wings…None of them seemed like foods a bear would like. What *did* a bear like to eat anyway? Salmon? Apples? Bamboo shoots? I hadn't seen any of them yet.

I was about to give up on the idea of getting the meter past 99 percent when a voice said, "Silica, here."

Sinon had snuck up behind me and offered a blue pot the size of a fist. I couldn't begin to guess what was inside. But Sinon had started in a different location and crossed the vast Giyoru Savanna on her own. I could only put my faith in her.

Silica accepted the jar, stuck her hand directly inside, and scooped out the contents. It was a whitish semisolid blob. She couldn't throw it because it was soft, so she carefully approached the bear instead.

"Here, it's yummy," she whispered, extending her hand. The thornspike cave bear eyed it warily.

"*Gruh…*," it grunted, sniffing. But it didn't seem to have any further reaction. Sinon muttered "I guess it's not good enough in a raw state…"

That made sense to me. The thornspike cave bear might not have been a boss monster, but it was definitely a rare type, and it might require all of its food lures to be properly cooked or treated in some way. But how would you prepare that white blob?

A small shadow darted between me and Sinon. Out of the corner of my eye, it looked to be Yui's size, but it wasn't her. The figure had brown fur and a long, narrow tail—one of the Patter. The leader of the group, if I recalled.

The Patter rushed with true rodent speed toward Silica and tilted the yellow jar she held over Silica's hand. A viscous golden liquid dolloped over the white object. Once that was done, the Patter raced back to the rear just as fast.

"……?"

Sinon and I stared, mouths agape. And then—the thornspike cave bear sniffed the object again and licked up the bizarre glob resting on Silica's hand in one slobbery go.

Her other hand moved immediately, draping the long rope around the bear's thick neck and forming a loop that she tugged shut. The thornspike cave bear's body flashed—and the crimson ring cursor turned green.

In the silence that followed, Silica slumped to the ground.

"*Hrar*!" the bear barked and licked her cheek with a massive tongue.

Behind me, I heard a voice ask, "Was it...a success?"

It was Alice. Even at night, the sapphire blue of her eyes lost none of its brilliance, though her eyes looked skeptical now. I couldn't necessarily believe it myself, but the cursor had undeniably gone from red to green.

"I think...it was."

"I did not believe this would work. Perhaps Silica has the skill to tame a wild dragon from the western empire."

"We'll have to take her to the Underworld one day to test that idea out," I replied before looking to Sinon. "So, uh...what was that white thing?"

"Butter."

"B-butter?! Where did you get *that*?!"

"An Ornith child gave it to me."

"......Oh..."

I shook away the confusion and glanced over my shoulder at the Patter.

"...And what did that mouse kid put on the butter?"

"Dunno." Sinon shrugged.

It was Yui who answered, approaching with her hand in Asuna's. "I think that's honey, Papa."

"H-honey?! Where did they...?"

"Long, long ago, the Patter collected honey from the Giyoru Savanna. Apparently, that honey is a treasure that was handed down in their clan for hundreds of years."

"Really? That was honey with a vintage of centuries? Why did they give us something so valuable...?" I asked, glancing back at the Patter again.

Yui said, "I didn't ask them. Should I?"

"It's probably best not to do that," Asuna said with a smile before I could answer. "You wouldn't want people asking you *why* you saved someone, would you?"

"Well...I suppose that's a good point..."

Though usually I'm the one getting saved, I thought. Kuro rubbed its head against my hip and yowled in a way that sounded suspiciously like a knowing chuckle.

"Well, if that was the case, I can see how it helped us tame that bear!" Leafa said.

Lisbeth gave her a funny look. "Why do you say that?"

"I mean, it's honey and butter! It's an irresistible combination!"

"Maybe for you," I murmured, except my stomach chose that very moment to gurgle loudly. Agil and Klein burst out laughing, and the girls all joined in.

In the end, we never got the chance to find out why Schulz's group was attacking the log cabin.

But if it happened twice, it was bound to happen three times. And we all agreed that the third time was likely to be much bigger than the first two.

So we only briefly celebrated reuniting with Sinon, Agil, and Klein and sat around a campfire in the front yard of the cabin to discuss the topic of defense.

At the southwestern end of the walled yard, the thornspike cave bear, Misha (named by Silica), was slumbering on its side with Kuro and Aga fast asleep on its luxurious-looking stomach fur. It was such a peaceful sight that it was hard to believe there'd just been a devastating battle on the other side of the wall. If we somehow lost our tamed status on Misha due to lack of food, that hellish scene would repeat itself, so once our meeting was over, we needed to leave at once to look for some food a bear would like.

The twenty Patter were resting in the living room of the log cabin. But we needed to be in a safe location to log out safely, too, so we'd have to build a new structure for them at some point. As usual, there were tons of things to do. But for now…

"Gotta beef up this wall, right?" Klein said, spreading his arms. "And make it twice as tall."

Alice nodded. "That last group scaled the wall without fear.

We'll need one tall enough to cause serious damage if they fall off. And we'll also want to flatten out all the divots and lumps on the outside surface."

I had to fight to resist grinning, realizing that she was thinking of the ideal defensive structure: the chalk-white walls of Central Cathedral. Even then, I couldn't hide from the knight's sharp senses, and she fixed me with a piercing stare.

"You haven't said anything yet, Kirito. Don't you have an opinion?"

"Sorry, sorry. Just thinking," I murmured, bobbing my head and clearing my throat. "Well…I have no objection to strengthening our defenses, but I think there's going to be an eventual limit to what we can do in that regard. We can make the wall taller, but then they'll use ladders. And as players get to a higher level, they'll gain more kinds of ranged offense…"

"So how do you expect to defend this place, then?" Lisbeth snapped impatiently. I decided to offer the idea I'd been mulling over since the Patter asked to join our traveling party.

"Does it seem to you like the reason we keep getting attacked is because we're just one little player house isolated in the wilderness?"

"Huh? You want to build more houses?"

"Yeah. But not one or two. We'll build a town here."

"……"

Nine pairs of eyes stared at me in stunned silence.

Asuna was the first to speak. "Just constructing a lot of buildings doesn't make a town, Kirito. You need people to live in them."

"Well, the Patter are going to need homes, aren't they? If we build five or six for them, that should make it more town-like, right?"

"So you want to use them as a shield?" Sinon asked sharply.

I shook my head. "No, no, we'll keep them safe, too. It just means we might be using them to help puff ourselves up and make this location harder for other players to attack…"

I could see that my argument wasn't convincing my friends, whose expressions grew harder as I went on.

"After crossing half the Giyoru Savanna, I realized that we're blessed by lots of natural resources in this location. There's a nearly unlimited amount of stone and lumber for building houses here. Iron ore was our biggest problem, but now that Silica's tamed the thornspike cave bear, that solves the major difficulty there."

Leafa jumped in to ask, "Wait...the bear's not going to respawn?"

"It will if we defeat it, but not if we tame it, I bet. Because then it would mean we could harvest an unlimited army of unstoppable monsters. We could have ten giant bears fighting for us."

"I don't want to try that one again," protested Silica, shivering. Atop her head, Pina opened one eye and squeaked as though to say "*Agreed.*" We chuckled at that one.

"We can visit the cave again later to see if it's true about the respawning...but for now, I don't think it'll be too difficult for us to make more buildings. But the Patter alone won't be enough to fill out a whole town, so we'll need to scout out some more NPCs."

"The Bashin would be very reassuring to have on our side!" chirped Yui. Lisbeth nodded firmly. Convincing NPCs to move homes was unthinkable in any other VRMMO, but here, it felt like it was just a successful negotiation away. The Bashin would be great to recruit, but I was hoping for the Ornith birdpeople Sinon met on the western side of the Giyoru Savanna. Having a group of people skilled with muskets would make our defenses so much more formidable...

"But, Kirito," Agil said, causing me to spin around, "you're playing this game to beat it, right? If we're heading for the 'land revealed by the heavenly light,' we're going to have to leave this forest eventually."

To my embarrassment, I'd completely forgotten about that announcement until he pointed it out. I blinked a few times, then nodded quickly.

"Er...yeah...good point. But there's a big difference between leaving from a secure base of operations and just striking out from nothing. For one thing, we're all lugging around incredibly heavy inherited gear. If it has to stay in our inventory all the time, it's just cramping our carrying space. And if we're going to keep it in our home storage, we'll want to make sure that it's as secure as possible..."

The others considered this suggestion gravely. Sinon's Hecate II was the most significant of these, of course, but everyone's inherited weapons and armor were important to them. Sadly, I'd had to sacrifice my beloved Blárkveld to create our metal weapons, but I still had Excalibur, which had to be protected at all costs. I knew the others felt the same way about theirs.

"Well, I'm in agreement with Kirito's idea to build a town. What do the rest of you think?" Alice announced. The others all murmured their assent. With that established, she looked to me. "But if we're starting from the planning stage, it's going to be a major project. It could take a week, or even an entire month. What if there is a third attack before we're finished?"

"No!" I bounced to my feet and clenched my fist, causing my iron gauntlet to clank loudly. "It won't even take a week! It's eleven o'clock right now, so I'll have the basic plan for the town built by three o'clock! That's four hours!"

Alice squawked, "Huh?! Four hours?!"

Asuna smirked. "We're going to be short on sleep again."

Yui cheered, "Let's give it our all!"

10

It was 1:35 PM the next day, Tuesday, September 29th.

I stood on the Seibu Shinjuku express train, fighting off the sandman.

If possible, I would have loved to make good use of this time to zonk out and catch up on some sleep, but that wasn't possible—because sitting next to me was the mysterious new transfer student Tomo Hosaka, aka Argo the Rat. If I fell asleep and leaned on her shoulder or, even worse, drooled on her, I'd never live it down for years to come.

So instead, I was desperately fighting back against the power that compelled my eyelids to shut. A mirthful voice said, "You seem sleepy, Kiri-boy. Want some eye drops?"

"N-no, I'm good. And what is it with you and wanting to give people eye drops?"

"Not just anyone."

"Oh, okay...Well, why are you following me, then?"

"Hey, that's kinda cruel to say to the person who taught you the secret life hack to gettin' out of school without ditching, huh?"

"Hrmm..."

Well, she had me there.

To make the arrangement to be in Ginza by three o'clock—a task that was nigh impossible for a high schooler—I was planning, despite my reservations, to ditch fifth and sixth periods. But when I mentioned that to Argo before the start of school, she informed me that I could get out of afternoon classes by applying for a workplace visit with the school.

Of course, I'd need an electronic signature from the business to be visited, but I had the man who was summoning me whip up something for that. The school accepted the application, so I wasn't branded with being delinquent from class, although it didn't change the fact that I was missing lessons. If this ended up being a waste of time, I was going to make full use of it by stuffing myself to the gills with expensive cake.

"I hear ya had a hell of a time last night, huh? Your base got attacked by a huge raid party?" Argo asked me out of nowhere.

".........How did you know that?" I asked after a healthy pause.

"A player who was takin' part in it was tweetin' all kinds of details out. The account was private, but that means nothin' to the great Argo."

"No way..."

I was muttering about the player tweeting out details, of course, not about Argo's information-collecting ability. It wouldn't be long before every former *ALO* player still alive in *Unital Ring* knew about our base.

I stifled the urge to sigh and replied, "Yeah, it was a hell of a thing. They were intending to wipe out our base from the very start. We managed to make it through because they didn't have magic, but if they had two or three mages, we would have lost." I paused, then considered what I had just said. "In fact...how *did* they have so many players, and none of them with magic? There should have been a bunch of players who inherited magic skills at the start of the game..."

"Ya can't use magic skills just by inheriting them into the game."

"Huh? Really?"

"The skill will show up in yer list of acquired skills, but it's inactive. Ya gotta use a magicrystal to unlock it. Once people figured that out, they went crazy looking for monsters that drop magicrystals around the Stiss Ruins starter area."

"Uh...uh-huh," I replied awkwardly. Then I hastily added, "But isn't that putting a huge handicap on magic classes? You might as well be beginning without any skill head start at all."

"I agree with ya. But if they didn't put any limitations, the magic skills woulda been way overpowered, I bet. It'd mean that in those first four hours before the grace period wore off, you'd have all the top-class devastating magic spells at your disposal, ya know? They could power-level on tough mobs and waste all the other players."

"Ahhh...Yeah, I get that..."

The MP recovery probably wouldn't allow for unlimited magic blasting, but if you gained enough levels, that wouldn't matter anymore. Like Argo said, if they hadn't placed those limitations, *Unital Ring* would likely be a mage-centric battleground by now. But even still, having to find and eat a magicrystal after your skill proficiency was lowered to 100 seemed a bit too restrictive to me.

The express train arrived at Kami-Shakujii Station, dropped off just a few passengers, then began moving again. Knowing the morning and evening rush hours, I had trouble imagining how these cars could be so empty. The afternoon sunlight shone through the windows and created a lattice pattern on the floor. Relaxing on the bench seating was making me sleepy again.

Ultimately, I stuck around until five last night—er, this morning. I did my best to live up to my promise to create the town in four hours, but it took one hour to gather the materials for the well, then another hour to find the plants to make our crop fields, and that just delayed the rest of the plans further.

But we worked hard together and managed to create something that resembled a town—at least, by video game standards.

We'd cut down parts of the forest outside the fifty-foot walled perimeter (which was easy because most of those trees had burned in the attack) and created another circular wall, dividing the interior into four separate areas. The eastern area was the living quarters for the Patter, the western area would be for future NPC settlers, the southern area was for commerce, and the northern area would be fields and pet stables. The western area was just a stone foundation for now, and there wasn't a single shop in the southern area yet, but it was looking much more like a town already. It wasn't until Alice pointed it out that I realized the circular four-quarter construction was exactly the same structure as Centoria in the Underworld—though our town was only two hundred feet across, smaller than a single district in the city of North Centoria.

Even still, in a single night, we managed to whip up an erstwhile town that was much better than I'd envisioned, much of which was thanks to Silica's new partner, Misha. Asuna used her Tailoring and Woodworking skills to fashion a large beast pack for Misha, giving it a seemingly infinite carrying ability for all the stone and logs we needed. Of course, the harder you worked a pet, the more its SP bar drained, so acquiring enough food to keep it going was an issue. But thanks to a fishing net that Asuna made and some additional proficiency in the Net-Casting skill, the river to the south actually started turning up some good-sized fish. Aga and Kuro loved the grilled fish, too, so that was a good solution to the problem of feeding our pets for now.

After that, the only question was whether this would create a sense of aversion and intimidation among the players who were likely to try attacking us in the future again. I certainly wouldn't ever want to do something like that, but some people might only find it a more enticing target this way, so we would just have to wait and find out. Perhaps there were new attackers sneaking toward our town at this very moment, while I was being rocked to sleep by the train.

The problem is this Sensei character...

I rested my head against the pole at the end of the seat, thinking about the player who *might* be behind the string of invasions.

The evocation of a teacher of PvP (PK) tactics made me think first of PoH, leader of Laughing Coffin, the murderous guild in Aincrad. But his fluctlight had been irrevocably damaged in the Underworld, so it was hard to imagine him showing up in *Unital Ring* and getting involved with PKing for fun. Plus, the whole mental instruction about "grasp the whole, not just one part" was not PoH's style. What he taught was how to lie and mislead people and give them poisoned water to drink.

So who was this Sensei…?

"Hey, Argo," I said. Her head was resting on my left shoulder, and it rose with a grunted "Nwuh? Wh-what…?"

"That locked account you saw. Did they say anything about *why* they attacked our base?"

"Hmm? No reason…I think the most he wrote was that a salamander friend of his invited him."

"Uh-huh…"

The salamander in question had to be Schulz. Which meant that he might have been the only person in contact with this Sensei.

Kirito…you're…really…

Those were Schulz's last words before he left the game for good. It had been an entire night since he said them, but I still had no idea what was supposed to come after "really." Of course, Schulz wasn't really dead, so it was possible I could use real-world means to make contact and hear what he meant to say…

"Hey, Argo."

"I'm gonna start charging you for my services."

"I'll buy you an expensive piece of cake in Ginza. Anyway…you have any idea what player in *ALO* might go by the title Sensei?"

"Yep."

I was stunned. The last thing I expected her to do was say yes.

"A-are you serious?" I asked, staring between those curls at her face.

"Yep. Though they usually call you the Black Swordsman, instead."

"……"

I snorted. It was certainly an answer but not the one I wanted.

"Forget that guy. Anyone else come to mind?"

"Hmm," she murmured but eventually shook her head. "Nope. Can't think of one. Seems like a number of *ALO* players who converted into *UR* have formed new teams of their own, so it could be the leader of one of 'em. I'd have to look into it to find out."

"When you say 'teams,' you mean like a guild?"

"A bit looser than that. More like groups based around sharing intel. They make up silly names, like the Absolute Survivor Squad, or the Announcer Fan Club, or the Weed Eaters, or the Virtual Study Society…"

"Yeah, those are pretty goofy…Anyway, can you look up who's leading those groups?"

"That's gonna cost ya more than a single piece of cake." Argo pouted, though her cheeks looked strange without the characteristic whiskers painted on.

"Hang on, Argo. At the meeting yesterday, you said you hadn't logged in to *Unital Ring* yet. How do you know so much about what's going on inside?" I asked.

"If you're thorough about collecting all the information being traded online, you can figure out most things. Back in the *SAO* days, I had ta walk around and collect all of that myself. Nowadays it's so much easier, I'm back to gaining weight," she joked, but it was clear to see beneath her jacket and uniform that her torso was just as skinny as it had been in *SAO*. I wanted to call her bluff and tickle her stomach but had to remind myself that she wasn't just the androgynous Rat anymore but a young woman one year above me in high school.

"Buuut," she drawled, "I'll admit that I'm thinkin' of loggin' in at last. Will you offer me an armed escort from the start point to your base, Kiri-boy?"

"Well…I did want to check out what the Stiss Ruins look like, so I guess that's fine…"

"Great! Tonight, then!"

It seemed like today's adventure was going to be another long one, I realized, looking up at the information panel over the train doorway. We'd just left Saginomiya Station.

We got off at Takadanobaba Station, changed lines, then finally reached Ginza, where the streets were bustling, despite its being a weekday. There were rich ladies in fine clothing and foreign tourists all over, which made me feel the slightest bit out of place in my school uniform.

We marched down the main street, its sides bristling with flagship stores of expensive luxury brands, and entered a distinctive red building at an intersection on the seventh block. The place we were heading was on the third floor. When we got off the elevator, the classical music playing made it immediately clear what a fancy place we were visiting, but I used my Incarnation power to dispel its intimidation before walking through the door.

"Welcome. Table for two?" asked a waiter, bowing deeply. I told him we were meeting someone and glanced around the spacious café.

From a window-side table in the back came a loud, impolite voice. "Hey! Kirito! Over here!"

I wanted to grab him and demand, *Are you doing this on purpose?!* Instead, I quietly hurried across the floor toward the source of the voice.

It was still five minutes to three o'clock, but the man with the dark-brown suit, flashy striped tie, and black-framed glasses was already half-finished with his fruit sandwich.

The first time I'd met Seijirou Kikuoka, he was a member of the Ministry of Internal Affairs; the next time, he was a lieutenant colonel of the Self-Defense Force; and now, I had no idea what he was, besides being the sketchiest person I knew by far. He grinned and raised a hand in greeting—but when he saw Argo standing next to me, his grin vanished, and he blinked in surprise.

"Hmm...Well, take a seat for now."

We sat across from him while the waiter set down glasses of cold water for us. Kikuoka exhaled, grumbling.

"So if this isn't Asuna or Suguha or Shino...who is this young lady, Kirito?"

But before I could open my mouth, Argo smirked and replied, "I believe you already know me quite well. At last we meet, Chrysheight."

(To be continued)

Unital Ring Abilities List

■ **Brawn:**	Bonus to medium- and large-melee-weapon damage, equip weight, and carry weight
■ **Bonebreaker:**	Bonus to damage that ignores enemy guarding
■ **Assault:**	Damage bonus to additional strikes during consecutive attacks
■ **Ironbreaker:**	Increased damage to enemy armor when attacking
■ **Bloodshed:**	Provides a chance to inflict Bleeding status when attacking
■ **Expand:**	Increased span of area attacks
■ **Repercussion:**	Inflicts minor damage on extra enemies in the vicinity of attack target
■ **Stupor:**	Provides a chance to inflict Stupor status when attacking
■ **Stout:**	Decreased knockback when guarding
■ **Rebound:**	Bonus to enemy knockback chance when guarding
■ **Chipped:**	Increased damage to enemy weapons, fangs, and claws when guarding
■ **Trip:**	Provides a chance to inflict Topple status when attacking
■ **Reflect:**	Reflects minor damage on enemy when guarding
■ **Terror:**	Provides a chance to inflict Terror status when attacking
■ **Drain:**	Provides a chance to restore MP when attacking

● **Toughness:**	Bonus to HP, TP, SP, and status-ailment resistance
● **Perseverance:**	Bonus to damage-reduction when guarding
● **Vitality:**	Additional bonus to HP
● **Chiseled:**	Bonus to base defense value
● **Invigoration:**	Bonus to HP regeneration rate
● **Taunting:**	Bonus to hate value accrued when attacking
● **Outburst:**	Provides a chance to inflict Frenzied status when attacking
● **Lethargy:**	Provides a chance to inflict Dull status when attacking
● **Antivenom:**	Bonus to damage-reduction
● **Resistance:**	Bonus chance to resist negative status ailment
● **Indomitable:**	Decreased movement penalty when over-encumbered
● **Purify:**	Bonus to status-ailment recovery speed
● **Stoicism:**	Provides brief period of movement after TP or SP reach zero
● **Gluttony:**	Can recover past maximum SP value when eating
● **Retention:**	Reduced rate of TP decrease

◆ **Sagacity:**	Bonus to MP value and magic power
◆ **Concentration:**	Bonus to MP recovery rate
◆ **Potency:**	Additional bonus to magic power
◆ **Maximize:**	Increased span of area magic
◆ **Streamline:**	Provides a chance for single-target magic attacks to penetrate target
◆ **Enlightenment:**	Decreased MP cost of magic
◆ **Blessing:**	Increased effect of healing magic
◆ **Consecration:**	Adds additional holy damage to weapon attacks
◆ **Learned:**	Increased proficiency gain of all language skills
◆ **Decipher:**	Increased proficiency gain of Ancient Writing skill
◆ **Esoteric:**	Increased proficiency gain of Ancient Magic skill
◆ **Practicality:**	Increased effect of consumable items
◆ **Keen Eye:**	Bonus to success rate of Identification skill
◆ **Artisan:**	Increased proficiency gain of all crafting skills
◆ **Insightful:**	Increased amount of harvested materials

- **Swiftness:** Bonus to ranged-weapon damage, small-melee-weapon damage, and jumping distance
- **Dexterous:** Bonus to ranged-weapon accuracy and lock-picking chance
- **Vital Aim:** Bonus to critical rate when attacking with ranged or small-melee weapon
- **Knockout:** Provides a chance to inflict Fainting status when attacking
- **Hamstring:** Provides a chance to inflict Crippled status when attacking
- **Adroit:** Bonus to armor-piercing chance when attacking with ranged or small-melee weapon
- **Chaining:** Bonus to consecutive-attack chance when attacking with small-melee weapon
- **Deadeye:** Additional bonus to ranged-weapon accuracy
- **Gallop:** Reduced rate of SP and TP decrease when running
- **Sprint:** Increased running speed
- **Shake Off:** Increased chance of losing targeted status when running
- **Concealment:** Bonus to success rate of Hiding skill
- **Acrobat:** Lowered weight, bonus to wall-run success
- **Hurdling:** Additional bonus to jumping distance
- **Landing:** Decreased damage when falling from heights

AFTERWORD

Thank you for reading *Sword Art Online 23: Unital Ring II.*

First off, I'd like to apologize for the strange publishing structure, that after Volume 21, *Unital Ring I*, Volume 22 was *Kiss and Fly*, only to continue with *Unital Ring II* here. We considered making *Kiss and Fly* a standalone short story collection so that this book could be Volume 22, but since Volumes 2 and 8 are also collections, I couldn't help but want to preserve that consistency with the series. Sorry about the interruption!

Anyway…it's taken a year, but here is the continuation of the *Unital Ring* arc. The last one ended with the production of iron, so I wanted our goal at the end of this book to be getting the whole group back together, but to my surprise, we shot past that right into creating a town. But only in the sense of clearing the land and putting down buildings. How Kirito and friends will function as a town and what that will mean for getting ahead in the game is something I'd like to elaborate upon in the next volume.

I wrote this volume in August and September 2019, for the most part, but at the time in the anime, the latter half of the *Alicization* season, the War of the Underworld, was just getting started. In that part of the story, Alice was tucked away in the distant Rulid Village, taking care of Kirito in his comatose state, working as a lumberjack to make a living, and chasing off Eldrie. I couldn't help but be aware of the huge gap between Alice there and in the *Unital*

Ring arc! However, on the inside, she's just the same as she was in the Underworld: always giving everything she's got. That mental strength will make her a pillar of Kirito's team going forward, I'm sure.

And with the introduction of that bespectacled fellow at the very end, it sure feels like the Underworld is going to get involved in the story again! What's going on in the human realm and the dark realm? I'm curious to find out, too, so I'm hoping to be able to depict that next time. But the world of *Unital Ring* demands constant attention, so we'll just have to see if that happens. I'll do my best to make sure it doesn't take an entire year for the next book!

On the personal side, for the first time in about five years, I'm back on my bicycle. The first time I tried to climb the side of a riverbed, my legs screamed bloody murder at me, but after a few months, I can make it up without losing much speed at all. The human body is a wonder. I'd like to keep up with that habit. Also, my schedule getting crunched to the last minute had nothing to do with my bicycle; it was simply the laws of the universe at work. I'm sorry, editor and abec!

Reki Kawahara—October 2019